For:
Denise DuBois
→ A lonely
Colleague —
Jeanne Wakefield Burke

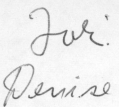

FRÄULEIN LILI MARLENE

and other stories

Sketches for the
following stories
by Franz Haacken:

"Fräulein Lili Marlene"
"The Painted Doodle Bug"
"The Superman" • *"Lilo"*
Remainder by H. Krause

Appreciation is hereby expressed to the following publications for per-
mission to reprint stories contained in this book: *Esquire* Magazine,
Charm, Flying, Real, Everybody's Weekly—Philadelphia *Inquirer, Carrafour*
(Paris) , *Idag* (Stockholm)

JAMES WAKEFIELD BURKE

FRÄULEIN
LILI MARLENE

and other stories

WORLD WIDE PRODUCTIONS

First printing	September, 1953
Second printing	October, 1953
Third printing	November, 1953
Fourth printing	December, 1953
Fifth printing	February, 1954
Sixth printing	March, 1954
Seventh printing	May, 1954
Eighth printing	August, 1954
Ninth printing	September, 1954
Tenth printing	October, 1954
Eleventh printing	January, 1955
Twelfth printing	March, 1955
Thirteenth printing	May, 1955
Fourteenth printing	September, 1955
Fifteenth printing	May, 1956
Sixteenth printing	August, 1956

For

James Richard Burke

FOREWORD

MEN MUST SPEAK out to one another, and when they believe deeply they speak boldly. In telling my stories I am not infrequently accused of speaking out too boldly. Some timid readers have said of me that I seek to transcend Henry Miller and Frank Harris. A prodigious ambition, if an inelegantly fatuous one. To these over-generous jobations I reply with the man who was ridden out of town on a rail: if it wasn't for the honor of it, I would just as soon walk.

An honest writer cannot confine himself only to the virtuous or reasonable or optimistic. It is his duty to hold a mirror up to life itself; he must portray an accurate and honest account of the deeds (and misdeeds) of his fellow man. This is an attempt at art, it is not "boldness," nor is it merely craftsmanship. It has been the case from Homer to Poe, from Swift to Hemingway. Otherwise there would have been no Boccaccio, Flaubert, Maupassant, Dostoyevsky, Hawthorne, Lawrence, Dreiser, Wolfe, Farrell, etc.

When he puts the critics above his own honest convictions, the writer finds himself trying too hard to "please" the public and appease his critics, and then he is in danger of becoming a superficial and dishonest writer. As Heywood Broun said, "It is good to keep an open mind, but it must not become a cave of the winds."

It is unfortunately characteristic of most modern writers that they have lost, to varying degrees but most to a serious degree, the epic art. The epic art is neither mysterious nor subtle; on the contrary, it constitutes perhaps the highest degree of simplicity. "Tell us a story," is the demand; and the story-teller obeys. Outside of and above his story, he is, in the simplest sense of the word, a reporter. If the story-teller is an honest reporter he will likely achieve a good story. I should like, and continually strive, to belong to that rare group of story-tellers.

I have not written the stories in this book to become beloved. I have put them down on paper from a deep and sincere sense of urgency—and I trust with integrity. I have lived among the members of the occupation, the soldiers and their Fräuleins, and among the German people since the end of the war, and feel that I am entitled to briefly hold the mirror up to their behavior, their deeds and misdeeds. I am a reporter. I have tried to give an honest picture of what the mirror caught. I can do no less; to do more would be stepping through Lewis Carroll's fanciful looking-glass. And I would not presume to set my dirty feet in Mr. Carroll's immaculate and transfigured world.

JAMES WAKEFIELD BURKE

CONTENTS

FRÄULEIN LILI MARLENE

The idea for the story "Fräulein Lili Marlene" first came to me in the early days of the war. I had not at that time ever heard of the song called "Lilli Marleen." I wrote a three-thousand word story dealing with a young girl who, unrooted from family and hometown and swept along by the restless tempo of war, finally fell into a life of semi-prostitution. Later, when I came to Europe and saw so many living examples of my Lili Marlene, I began to realize that I had perhaps done my character a grave injustice in portraying her as I had done. So I rewrote the story, attempting to justify her deeds in the light of the cruel forces of war and to show that the blame for the steps down she had taken was not entirely her own. It is my belief that the story of Fräulein Lili Marlene has a common denominator with all the people throughout the world in any way touched by the war. The story pretends to be a record, told through the eyes of Lili Marlene, of the desires, aspirations and struggles of all these girls, in essence, a record of their profoundest experiences. If we can rely on the Old and New Testaments, nothing that comes from the deep, passional soul is bad, or can be bad. Therefore I make no apologies for Lili Marlene.

JAMES WAKEFIELD BURKE

He begged her not to tell his elder brother about his indiscretion . . .

FRÄULEIN LILI MARLENE

LILI MARLENE came back to Almfurt early one spring morning before the little Bavarian town had awakened. She had come back to marry Karl Ingolmann, who was home from a Russian prison camp. Karl Ingolmann had been Lili Marlene's childhood sweetheart, and when he went away to war she had promised to wait for him. But Karl had been reported missing in action, presumed dead; and, swept along by the wave of restlessness that unroots non-combatants, she had gone to Berlin.

Lili Marlene came back to Almfurt on a wheezing, struggling old Diesel bus, which miraculously arrived an hour before the train on which Karl expected her. After telegraphing Karl from Berlin, she had discovered she did not quite have the train fare. She alighted from the bus and went across the cobblestone street toward a *Gasthaus*, rummaging in her purse for coins with which to telephone Karl.

The men standing around the bus craned their necks and followed her with their eyes, for Lili Marlene was a girl whose appearance at once arrested men. She paid absolutely no attention to them, for she had long ago discovered that her physical composition was parent to the glint in every man's eyes, that it was as natural for the gaze of the male to follow her as for the wings of the moth to fly toward the flame. In Berlin the Americans whistled whenever she passed by—if indeed she got by. The British daringly invited her to tea. The French saluted and accosted her with bold compliments. The Russians —well, she simply kept out of their reach. The German men, given to seeing all things as either black or white and with their eternal *Herrenvolk* attitude toward the distaff, approached her as a girl to be entwined to their desires as a vine to the limb. Lili Marlene, however, maintained a level indifference of the lustful attentions men turned on her, and disdained to make use of the tokens of her voluptuousness to arouse the male.

No single feature of the girl seemed responsible for her provocative beauty, but rather each lineament was a complimentary attribute to her over-all comeliness: the light hair that flowed in gentle waves almost to her shoulders: the straight, high-bridged nose that lent a commanding attractiveness to the face: the eyes, like globes of cobalt, that, from under long lashes, looked confidently upon the world: the mouth which was full and mobile and about which eternally hovered the ghost of a smile, not the polite smirk of a girl conscious of the desire she provoked in men, but a soft flutter which moved with her eyes and made something tender and sweet, something vaguely reminiscent of the Lili Marlene who had years ago left Almfurt, surge to the surface of her whole daring face.

Lili Marlene, unlike most Bavarian girls, had a narrow waist and smooth shapely legs, made sharply meaningful by dark, sheer nylons. Her bosom, however, was traditionally Bavarian: abundant, high breasts rose and strained at their gauzy confines with her every breath and movement. Her clothes were tasteful, if not expensive, and the smooth curving lines of her figure gave them an extremely smart appearance. Underneath a three-quarter-length coat she wore a trim navy blue suit and her small feet were encased in smart high-heeled American-made shoes. An off-the-face hat with a red crown and a white rim rode aft on her head, which was always held high and straight ahead.

Lili Marlene was about to make her call when she changed her mind, dropped the two ten-Pfennig coppers back in her purse, and went out of the *Gasthaus* toward Kirchplatz, which was the center of the town. It would be easier, she decided, to return slowly and naturally to this private haven of her dream, the one dream she had kept alive and safe while the world cruelly and crazily murdered everything else about her. She crossed the Bahnhofstrasse, her sharp heels cautiously picking their way over the damp, round tops of the ancient cobbles. Over the gently rising stone bridge, across the little river, and she was on Fürstenstrasse, the main thoroughfare of Almfurt. She passed Wendel's Hardware Store. What a difference! When she went away the windows were filled with "scenery" —potted plants, cardboard illustrations, a few old repaired implements. Now there was everything: bright new pots and pans, stoves and baked enamel bathroom fixtures, lamps and electrical gadgets, radios and playing machines, rolls of wire and rope, lengths of chain—everything to satisfy man's needs and whims. There was old Frau Potts' *Konditorei*. It was literally loaded with chocolate and icing-laden cookies, sweet buns bursting with rich filling, cakes with spacings of creamy sweets and covered with whorls of thick, white whipped cream. She passed the post office, the music store, its windows glistening with new instruments. She saw familiar *Bier* and *Wein* signs advertising places whose interiors she had never seen; whose likenesses, however, she had become thoroughly familiar with since leaving Almfurt. It was all wonderful, these streets and scenes of her happy childhood. But soon the thrill faded and thoughts of Berlin came through—and made her wince. Before she went away life had been simple and understandable, even kindly, in spite of the stringencies of war. Now life was complex and pressing, beset with confusion and ofttimes painful.

It promised to be a lovely day. The eastern sky, frothy with apple colors, smiled down on the large oval of stores built around the towering old church whose massive walls, steep roofs and pointed arches were darkened with centuries of rust and dust. The place was deserted, save for two men who were unloading vegetables and huge slabs of meat at the front entrance of Kutscher's Restaurant. She thought of the contrast between this active little town, busily waking up to its morning duties, the streets filling gradually with people freshly washed and walking briskly, and the life in Berlin, with nobody about at this hour but the street-cleaners and others who serviced the teeming city while its luckier occupants still slept. "So early!" Lili Marlene said to herself. "If I were back in Berlin I'd still be in my bed." She winced at the thought of Berlin and it was like a knife plunged deep and quick. She had to forget all about Berlin and her life there—if she could.

She went across and entered Kutscher's Restaurant for a cup of coffee. The night manager was yawning and watching the wall-clock, impatient to be relieved. When Lili Marlene entered the place he became alive and all at once attentive. He came immediately to the table where she sat down. She recognized the signs and said, "Coffee, please," before he got around to getting fresh with her.

The manager drew the coffee, all the while casting glances over his shoulder and trying to catch her with a smile. She ignored him completely. When he brought her coffee his eager eyes devoured her. She noticed that he had red hair and his skin was covered with freckles like so many copper pfennig pieces. His loose, greedy mouth twisted in a smile. He asked, intoning the question roguishly, "Stranger in Almfurt?"

She sipped her coffee, inhaled its nutty odor, and gave him a smiling look. "I came in from Berlin just now."

"Berlin!" he repeated eagerly, and as if the word had been an invitation for him to assume familiarities, pulled out a chair and sat down. "Ah, Berlin! I'll bet they appreciate you in Berlin. I'll bet the fellows up there call you 'Peaches-and-cream.' "

She halted him with her wide, dark blue eyes. He flushed, recovered, gave her a rascally grin. "Look, Peaches-and-cream," he said in an intimate tone, "I'll be off in half an hour, and then my time is yours—all yours, from then on."

The two looked into each other's eyes: the girl scolding without scorn, the redhead scenting a pick-up. "No, thanks," Lili Marlene said. She paid for the coffee and left.

When she went out the door, he called after her. "Too bad, Peaches-and-cream! It would have been fun. See that convertible standing at the side of the church? It's mine. I often drive up to Berlin."

Lili Marlene walked around the church, wondering what to do until the train on which Karl expected her would arrive. She sat down on one of the age-stained stone benches. Seeing Almfurt again, coming home after so long a time, had touched her emotionally, brought up the past in her memory. Reminiscences were rushing up from the vaults of her memory and tumbling in her head. She opened her purse, got out a cigarette, lit it and smoked it halfway, then dropped it on the stones and ground it beneath her feet. Her memories were becoming organized now, sharp and clear; and for the next half hour she sat there like a dreaming sylph, reliving them all, most with a certain pleasure, some with sadness, and a few with regret.

She thought of Karl, and the days of their childhood. They had been neighbors and, in the accidental way of life, had grown up together as neighboring children do. She remembered the schooldays together: the long slanting rays of the sun streaming in on the sleepy afternoon one-room class: the drone of the teacher's voice lulling them to sleep: Karl breaking the monotony by tying scraps of paper into her braids, throwing spitballs at her. The way home after school: she and her girl friend, Eva, giggling and running and sharing the mysterious, vital secrets of little girls: Karl running after them and throwing chestnuts from the September trees; then casually and indifferently coming alongside and walking them home. The sleigh rides in the still, frozen Bavarian winter, the Christmas carols, the ice-skating on the pond just outside the city. And the gift-giving season itself, with the three of them—somehow, she realized, it had really always been three of them—secretly consulting each other, and pretending to be surprised when, on the basis of their mutual consultations, each had gotten exactly what he wanted. And then she remembered the long, shivery but promising days of early spring: the Easter morning walks with their parents, the children impatient to get away for their own afternoon fun in the parks and woods. How long those years seemed, she thought, as though they would never end! How endless the summers had seemed, the summers when they had gone fishing together, or hiking through the Bavarian foothills, stopping to eat their lusty basket lunches beside the shady tinkling of a mountain brook that cascaded merrily down through the hills to join the distant Danube. Karl—Karl, serious Karl, Karl who knew everything—had told the two girls about the *Nöck,* the water-spirit who hid in the brooks and could be heard singing, if you listened carefully, behind a waterfall. And the two thirteen-year-old girls had listened seriously and carefully, straining their ears to hear the *Nöck,* and Eva had even once claimed that she heard him, whereupon Karl's eyes had twinkled. But Lili Marlene, although wide-eyed, envious and uncertain, had been too much a devotee of the truth to be able to join in Eva's assertion.

Now the kaleidoscope quickened, and the years started moving faster. She remembered the parties and the dances, with Karl always asking her, and Eva saying nothing, but her brown eyes narrowing.

And then there had been the Whitsuntide holiday before the war, when Karl and she had been going together for so long that it seemed only natural for them to become engaged.

And then it was October, and the whole family stood soberly at the little railway station in Almfurt. Karl and other boys of the town were going off to war. And Karl had held her tightly, as though he would not, could not, dared not let go. Then he had kissed Eva perfunctorily, and hugged his mother and father once more. As the train pulled slowly out, he leaned out of the window and managed to barely touch Lili Marlene's fingers lightly with his. And that was all.

Then had come the letters, the daily letters for which she lived. And one day they stopped coming, and instead there was a list at the *Rathaus* which included Karl's name among those who were missing.

Together with Eva she had left Almfurt—why should she stay in Almfurt now, waiting for what?—and gone to Berlin, a big city teeming with restless millions mobilized into a colossal nerve center of the war machine. There was work for everybody, even for a couple of green girls from a small Bavarian town. Lili Marlene got a job as a file clerk for Eckert & Eckert, Attorneys, in the Friedrichstrasse. She and Eva took an apartment together. Eva got a job in the Propaganda Ministry. They hardly ever spoke of Karl, but both of them knew that something was missing from their lives.

Fate rushed in, very soon, to fill the vacuum.

Eckert & Eckert were brothers, both in their thirties. The elder was married to a woman of his own age named Else and had three tow-headed children. He had dark blond hair, a squarish face and a watermelon paunch. An active Party member, he was ambitious for a post in the hierarchy. And there was reason to believe he would realize his ambition: for his were the eyes of a young judge who dreams of senates, who stands forever through his dreams decrying in measured sentences the rascality of a thousand Semites. The younger Eckert was a bachelor, neither clever nor ambitious. His nose was prominent, his chin receding, his teeth bad, his hair was thin and he spread it carefully over his balding pate. Too often and too intimately he would lean over from behind Lili

Marlene to give her low-toned instructions. His rapacious eyes traveled over her in a way that gave her an embarrassed, uncomfortable feeling, as if she were being stripped piece by piece of all her clothes. Almost from the outset, both the Eckert brothers, each carefully concealing his design from the other, and each in his own way, began to make advances toward Lili Marlene.

The bachelor brother struck out boldly. Lili Marlene was obliging, grateful and, in a way, humble; so he had little trouble in enticing her to his apartment after office hours on the pretext of extra work. After a while of unceasing toil he would put a platter of forbidden Strauss on the electric player, open a bottle of wine, and repeat in his nasal voice, "Now, my dear, you must relax a little. You have worked quite hard tonight."

Green as Lili Marlene was at the time, she recognized the unmistakable signs. She would put the papers in order and say, with lowered eyes, "Thank you, Herr Eckert, but I really must go home."

"Of course, my dear," he would say, and with a twisted little sickening smile, hold her coat for her and escort her to the door, where he would try to fondle and kiss her before letting her depart.

Finally, overpowered one night by his own mounting desire, he flung his arms around her and began kissing her and would not let her go. She threatened to scream for the landlady and he relented. He begged her not to tell his elder brother about his indiscretion, making a coward's promise to henceforth behave himself, a promise which he was never quite able to keep.

Now at this time a love came into Lili Marlene's life. She was dining alone in Kempinski's cafe one night when Eva came in with a group of soldiers, whom she was patriotically entertaining. She saw Eva in a different light that night; it was a new Eva, an Eva in which a latent and brilliant warmth had come to the surface. Eva had always been pretty in a way, even attractive, but something was lacking, something of the not quite definable spark that characterized Lili Marlene had always been missing in Eva. That night there was a reason for Eva's new warmth. His name was Corporal Paul Halder, and Lili Marlene soon saw why Eva had fallen for him. In many ways he looked like Karl: the same mixture of youthfulness and seriousness, the same fair skin and dark hair, the same sympathetic smiles and gestures.

After dinner the whole group made the rounds of the nightclubs together. During the course of the evening Corporal Paul Halder was drawn more and more to Lili Marlene. It was she he danced with, she for whom he smiled and talked gaily. And he was for her like a fresh breeze out of the past: he brought the sweet nostalgia of Almfurt and home: he stirred her as had Karl. Eva was quick to notice their mutual affinity and her eyes narrowed in the old way, and when she had to leave shortly before eleven o'clock to report back to the Propaganda Ministry she was openly jealous and resentful of Lili Marlene. The evening ended with Corporal Halder walking Lili Marlene home in the gloom of the blackout. They went through the deserted streets, hand in hand, he wondering if she would let him see her again and she hoping he would ask.

Most of Paul's three week furlough was still left, and they saw each other constantly. She gave him her brightest smiles and her warmest kisses. Paul loved her: his soft brown eyes sang it: his sensitive mouth proclaimed it and his impressionable open face advertised it wantonly. And gradually he came to be everything to Lili Marlene. She thought only of him, looked forward anxiously to the appointed hour when she would meet him. He made her exquisitely happy. His avidity was tempered by his open, eager boyishness. He would grab her and smother her with kisses in public places, and when she protested he would laugh like a child and say, "I love you so much, my darling, I can't help it!" During meals he would take her hand under the table and hold it, whispering, *"Mein Liebling! Meine liebe* Lili Marlene!"* She would smile and look away, embarrassed, and plead impatiently but happily, "Please! Now eat, and let me eat!"

During these three weeks she found out what she had so devoutly hoped for—that she was in love with Paul.

The night of his departure Paul came to her apartment, intending to take her out for one last round of nightclubs and fun before he departed again for France and an uncertain future. She was changing into her prettiest dress when outside the sirens suddenly started wailing—a sudden, surprise air-raid, a nuisance raid, of the kind that were becoming frequent in those days. They looked at each other and a silent knowledge passed between them—that the sirens could not rob them of their last night together, and, as if by mutual agreement, they did not bother to get up and run for the air-raid shelter. The wailing of the sirens and the short, distant explosions as the planes dropped a brief cargo of death over the city was like ugly background music in her ears, compellingly reminding her of the past and the present and the future all at once. They remained there and talked. She told Paul of her childhood and her life with Karl. It was as if Karl himself were sitting opposite her. And she thought of Karl who had loved her and whom she had loved, and whom she had let go, with joy untasted, their love unconsummated. She thought of the still-raging war, and of the fact that Paul was going away on the morrow. An immense and genuine pity filled her; pity for herself, for their lives torn by the soulless machine of war; pity for all soldiers, all over the world, lying in trenches and commanded to kill; pity for Karl dead in an unnamed grave; pity for Paul. Then he tenderly kissed her, and when he put his arms around her and lifted her off her feet and carried her over to the bed, she did not resist, but gave herself to him willingly and gladly and happily. He left her in the pre-dawn

...oom. His face glowed as he gave her a last long warm embrace, and she kissed his eyes and let him go.

Life went on in the same old way now, with the bachelor Eckert still making his clumsy advances toward Lili Marlene. She thought of Paul, and looked upon Eckert with a mixture of loathing and pity.

The elder Eckert, however, nearly succeeded where the bachelor brother had failed. He took pains to learn Lili Marlene's whims and little pleasures and dislikes, and catered to them all. He tried to soften her up with gifts; they were numerous, frequent and sometimes expensive. One night he "accidentally" ran into her in Kranzler's Restaurant. He knew that she often went there after work to have a cup of ersatz coffee and dream of the days when there would be no more shortages. He smilingly pretended that it was an "unexpected" pleasure and invited her to join him. Where was Frau Eckert, she wanted to know. "Else? She seldom comes out at night any more. The bombings," he explained. "She doesn't like to leave the children. But I go out almost every night."

The serious lawyer was a completely different man away from the office. He tried hard to be gay and his efforts made him appear much younger. He looked for Lili Marlene every night at Kranzler's and the other places she might stop to eat before going home. He would join her, pay the check and walk her home or whenever they could find a cab in the busy, tight, war-bustling city, accompany her in that conveyance. Frequently, before going home, he would suggest that they stop by the Royal Club or the Adlon Bar or the Eden Cafe for a drink. Bit by bit he swept away all her resistance against going out with a married man. And so Lili Marlene saw Berlin night life, what was left of it in the last year or so of the war.

One night, while they were sipping brandy in a little bar off Kurfürstendamm, a terrible air-raid came. It came suddenly

and fearsomely: the buildings around them shook and groan
glass cracked and shattered: the very foundations of the stree
themselves seemed about to burst and heave up, as though the
violence were rumbling up from the bowels of the earth, instead of screaming down out of the sombre sky. They had been
overwhelmed by the suddenness of the raid. But when a breath-
ing-space came they picked their way hurriedly through the
rubble, the lurid glare of the fires caused by the bombs light-
ing up the city around them, and rushed into an air-raid shelter. For a long time she shivered with fright in a remote sec-
tion of the shelter, in Eckert's arms. It was dark in their corner
and they seemed to be all alone in the gloom, just the two of
them, with hell screaming and bursting and flaming outside.
He kissed her and held her powerfully and protectingly. She
never knew when she was no longer on her feet. Suddenly
they were sitting, their backs against the cold and reverberat-
ing cement wall, then she was lying on the concrete floor, close
in his arms. The bombs were exploding and clawing at her
from the outside: she pressed closer to Eckert. The mixture of
madness and passion and death was tumbling through her
blood. Instinctively she was reliving that delicious night with
Corporal Halder, when a similar but far, far smaller hell
roared outside. Eckert sensed the girl's crazed, unreasoning emotion and drew her to him, gently, but with a firm and determined purpose. And then the bombs stopped, the air-raid was
over, and a deathly quiet came. She looked at Eckert, and
thought of Paul. She turned from Eckert with distaste.

He brought her home, and when they came to her room he
tried to come in as a matter of course. She stopped him with
a cold look and closed the door against him. Next morning
she cleaned out her desk and left the offices of Eckert & Eckert,
Attorneys. She never saw either of them again.

For a time Lili Marlene hated all men. On those who looked
at her with amorous smiles she turned a cold back. With the

German war machine crumbling and the front reaching a chaotic stage, letters from Paul had become infrequent. She had no way of knowing whether he was still alive or not. She cherished the memory of their three weeks together and the last, despairingly happy night of his furlough. But there was no hope in her heart.

She got a job as receptionist and typist for Sethe & Sohn G. m. b. H. in a district of Berlin known as Spandau. Sethe & Sohn G. m. b. H. manufactured a small 7.65 caliber pistol which the SS officers used. Felix Sethe, son of the founder who had manufactured toy trains and had died in 1937, was the manager and he had a suburban home and a wife to whom he was unfaithful whenever he could arrange an occasion. He was a tall, bony man with yellow skin, and had a pointed chin and large tear-drop ears. His hound-dog face reflected rapacity, and his brown-flecked eyes burned with a thousand rascally schemes. Felix Sethe had a great many tools but a lie was the handle that fitted them all. He spoke softly, scarcely moving his bony jaws, and smiled with the tight skin of his face, affecting a great deal of charm, concealing a suspicious and malicious nature. Anyone could see by the way his sensual eyes followed Lili Marlene what he was wishing.

Lili Marlene, on guard and the wiser for her experience with the lawyers Eckert, remained aloof from him. When he asked her to go with him to Leipzig for the avowed purpose of entertaining some important Nazi industrialists, she agreed. It was, she thought, a duty connected with her job and the war. Felix Sethe met the industrialists with Lili Marlene, as he declared he would, and he and Lili Marlene entertained them and Sethe got the contract. When the party was over and the industrialists disposed of, Felix Sethe proposed to take Lili Marlene to her hotel in a taxi. It was the time of night when the city sounds are faintest, and a late moon languished in the lonely heavens. They rode for a long time. Lili Marlene

sank back in the cushions of the open-top cab, mellowed t
an immense loveable feeling from the champagne. The cab
wound through the suburban road, up and over low dark hills,
and finally drew up before an old castle which had been con-
verted into a wartime hotel.

Suddenly the stillness of the night was shattered as the now
too-familiar roar of crashing and screaming bombs met their
ears. A brace of explosives landed dangerously close to the
hotel: windows crashed and bricks flew from the old building.
They dashed for the open field. Her blood started pounding
in her ears, and again she felt the strange agitation and
turmoil. It was as if the imminent deathly danger, the vast
upsetting convulsions of the exploding bombs had released a
coiled and tense spring inside her: the thing seemed to whirr
round and round inside her, beating, stirring, flaying all sorts
of wild unreasoning emotions. She and Felix crouched on a
tiny hillside, ran as the bombs let up, fell flat as they exploded
dangerously nearby, got up, ran again. Finally they tumbled
in a grassy ravine, like two small children rolling playfully
together down a hillside. She was in his arms, underneath
him. She did not move. There was a wonderful sense of
safety and comfort there, with him between her body and the
death that stalked the land around them. Four powerful bombs
exploded in great jarring upheavals; then all was quiet. The
champagne started circling giddily in her head again. She
laughed a little hysterical laugh. It was over—over! The raid-
ers had gone. She wanted to scream with joy—or was it fright?
Why didn't Felix Sethe get up, let her up. Why didn't he
move? He *was* moving, with an urgency; he was clawing at her.
She laughed a little feverish laugh, then she sobbed. She had
a sense of pushing at him, fighting him away. He became
more urgent, and in a sort of vast indifference, compounded
of horror and the heady wine and the agitation and exhaustion, she yielded to him: she did not give in: she gave up.

Upon arriving back in Berlin, Lili Marlene was discharged by Felix Sethe's office manager without explanation.

Next day came the long awaited news of Paul, a telegram saying he was on his way to Berlin.

She met him at the station, full of love, excited, happy. He brought gifts with him: a large package in fancy wrappings, and a cute, ungainly puppy, which he placed on the table. It stood there on its wobbly legs, and—its first gesture which it was to repeat many times—licked Lili Marlene's outstretched fingers quietly and happily. She was overwhelmed with the gifts—a bottle of Guerlain's Mitsouka perfume, some exquisite silk lingerie, a delicate gold chain—but it was the dog that she took to her heart immediately.

That evening they went to a newsreel movie, and in the course of it there were some shots of Paris, the Arc de Triomphe, the Eiffel Tower. Suddenly she cried: "Eiffel! That's what we'll call him!" "Call whom?" said Paul bewilderedly. "The dog, of course," she answered, and squeezed his arm affectionately.

After a wonderful evening of wining and dancing they returned, hand in hand, two young people wondrously in love, through the darkened, still streets to Lili Marlene's apartment. It was a night that Eva would not be home: she had gone to Dresden on a mission for her chief. Eva, an ambitious girl, was making headway in the Propaganda Ministry. Paul took off his tunic, Lili Marlene hung it in the closet. They kissed with a gentleness that gathered force and passion, and then faded back into gentleness. She released herself tenderly. He went to the divan, and, lying on his back, smiled happily in the dimness of the room. As he knew she would, she came and sat beside him. Between them there was an unspoken willingness, an overpowering precedent experienced, a silent consent given. Yet there was a shadow between them, holding them apart. The shadow, seen only through Lili Marlene's eyes, was the shadow of the other men. She felt guilty with both Eckert and Sethe: guilty with Eckert because she had strangely wanted him to take her, and guilty with Sethe because she had let him take her. She wanted to put loathesome ghosts out of her mind, out of her heart. But she knew she could not. There was only one way: she had to tell Paul everything.

With a sort of defiance she began. She talked slowly, deliberately, in a monotone, without looking at Paul. She told about how she had resisted the younger Eckert, how she had let the elder Eckert win her confidence, how she felt when she lay in his arms in the air-raid shelter that night. She told him about Sethe. And as best she could she described her own feelings when it had happened. Then, after a long pause, she said, "Don't blame it on the bombings, on my hysteria. Paul, you must blame me. I could have stopped them. A girl can always stop a man—if she really wants to. I can only ask you to try and forget about it all, erase it from your mind, as I shall try to do. It is you I want, Paul, in the honest way every girl wants the man she loves."

Paul was stunned. Then, as realization dawned, he was incredulous. He stood up, avoiding her eyes, which were hopefully searching for a sign, a kindness from him. He paced the floor, desperately unable to overcome his hurt. Lili Marlene lying in the arms of another! It was a deep, poignant hurt: an actual pain, like a long, sharp knife plunged through his chest. She saw what he was enduring, and grieved at his suffering, almost sorry that she had told him, wishing with all her might that she could do something to cancel out the past and hoping against all hope that he would find it in his heart to forgive her.

Unable to bring himself to a decision and overpowered by the great shock to his sensitive emotions, he wandered out of the apartment, down the steps and into the dark street. She lay on the couch, looking into the gloom, her cheeks wet with tears and filled with a sense of finality—of doom—of complete abandonment—and with a dead coldness in her heart. It was over. He had left her. She was sorry she had had to tell him, but knew that she could not have done otherwise. She bitterly cursed the fate of war that had led her into these paths. And as if in threatening answer to her malediction the wail of an air-raid warning signal pierced the still night. She sat very quiet, waiting, waiting for the first explosions of the bombs. She was filled with a blankness, a nothingness, save for a cruel desperate desire for the bombs to hurry and fall. It didn't matter if she was caught by the very first one. Then she thought of Paul—Paul wandering about the streets. He would be killed! She sprang up and ran out of the apartment and down the stairs.

As she ran through the streets she heard the planes overhead. They had come in very high and in mass formation: the bombs, when they came, would blanket the city. There was no sign of Paul. She ran on, calling his name. The bombs began to rain down. They screamed and crashed and exploded around her. She went on, crying for Paul. Finally she saw him: he was nearly two blocks away. He was coming toward her. Then he saw her. His arms reached out toward her. He ran faster. She knew what was in his heart: he had won the struggle with himself and was coming back to take her in his arms and forgive her. Suddenly there came a wild screaming out of the heavens and the street, the buildings—the world itself—burst in a mighty upthrusting of concrete, fire, earth and fury. She was thrown, stunned, behind the corner of a building. A moment later she was forging her way through the stifling atmosphere of dust, fire and cordite burning in her throat and nostrils. Then she found Paul, his lifeless body pitifully mingled in the rubble.

Since arriving in Berlin Eva had become a new, a transformed woman: a woman of importance. With her rise in the

Propaganda Ministry she had taken on a becoming poise. She was constantly in the company of men, many of them important officials and bureaucrats, and she was eternally trying to thrust them onto Lili Marlene. Eva had learned, through secret communications inside the Ministry, that Karl was alive and held in a Russian prison camp. It is known that the Nazis sometimes withheld such information, after the next of kin had been notified to the contrary. This was the circumstance in Karl's case. Eva did not tell Lili Marlene about Karl; she still wanted him for herself. Still resentful over the loss of Paul, she hoped that by throwing a variety of men at Lili Marlene she could ruin her so that when Karl came back he would not want her.

Lili Marlene, however, was not interested in Eva's friends. After Paul's death she transferred all her affection to little Eiffel. She would spend long hours playing with him, teaching him new cute tricks, fondling and hugging him. He would lie on her bed, looking soulfully up at her, and lick her fingers, as he had done on the night Paul had brought him.

Eva got Lili Marlene a job as private secretary to Gerhard Spindler, a well-known newscaster. Gerhard Spindler was a wiry, jerky fellow with long dark hair, which, if he did not keep it combed and slicked carefully back, would hang shaggy-dog fashion over his ears. All the girls in the building had him tagged for what he was: an erotic, vain and pretentious would-be Don Juan. He was constantly telling and laughing at his own lewd jokes. He would pace ostentatiously up and down behind her, dictating his copy from teletype reports in his hand, while she took it down on the typewriter. Occasionally he would fall silent and she would feel his hand under her arm or over her shoulder trying to cup her breast or caressing her neck or patting her on the leg. But like him or not, Gerhard Spindler was in the know of things in Berlin.

It was known, when the Russians besieged the city, that the cause was lost. One night, when the city was slowly crumbling before the siege guns of the Red Army, Gerhard Spindler pulled Lili Marlene into a corridor and said, "You've got to get out of Berlin. The city is lost; it's only a matter of hours. I'm leaving. I have a way out. I can take you with me."

She had the choice of remaining in the doomed city or going with Gerhard Spindler. She quickly decided to go with him but made him promise to take Eva too. But when they got to her apartment the Russians had already been there. The place was a wreck, pillaged and upset. Little Eiffel was cowering under the bed, whimpering. There was no sign of Eva, and no time to look for her. Lili Marlene hastily discovered that her precious lingerie, which Paul had brought her, had not been looted. She threw it, together with a few necessities, into a small handbag, gathered up Eiffel and hastily left with Spindler.

He guided her safely to a field on the outskirts of the city, where he had hidden under a brush pile a *Tempowagen*, a small tricyle-type truck with a one-cylinder engine attached to the front wheel. They did not get far before the vehicle was commandeered by a straggling unit of the German army. Then they climbed aboard a boxcar attached to a slow-moving south-bound train.

The train dragged on, stopping, waiting, starting. Sometimes it stood for long hours without moving. Finally it moved out of reach of the Russians. It may have been the warm sun, or the slow tempo, or the burgeoning spring countryside, or merely his ineffable vanity that made Gerhard Spindler decide that it was time for Lili Marlene to pay up for "all that he had done for her." They were completely alone in the empty boxcar: there was nobody to stop him—except Lili Marlene. At his first clumsy embrace she shoved him disgustedly aside. The train gave a lurch and he half-fell, staggered to the other side of the car.

With the power of instant decision, to which she had in recent years become accustomed, she took Eiffel under one arm, her precious overnight case in her hand, and leaped off the train. As she looked back she saw the infuriated Spindler looking angrily after her. "You ungrateful wench!" he yelled.

After days of wandering over the countryside, trying to discover what to do, where it would be safe to go, she struck out in the general direction of Bavaria. Across field and over fence, she finally came to the autobahn. This once-jammed artery, a product of German ingenuity, was now a lonely double strip of concrete winding its way across a deserted and still countryside. It would eventually take her to Bavaria. Occasionally, as she walked, sometimes carrying Eiffel under her arm and sometimes letting him trot along at her feet, she would come to the twisted wreckage of a bridge, which the once-mighty *Wehrmacht* had destroyed in hasty retreat towards Berlin. She and Eiffel would pick their way across jagged concrete and broken steel or wade across shallow streams. She had made up her mind. She would go home to Almfurt. Home. That was the place to go; and sometimes as she trudged tiredly on she would repeat it over and over again: Almfurt—home: Almfurt—home.

The hours passed, and the stops for rest became frequent. Her state of irritation and depression grew as she noted that the sole of one of her shoes, not built for this kind of cross-country endeavor, had come loose. She sat down and wearily pulled off her shoes and began rubbing her aching feet. A quick shadow flashed in the bushes across the concrete strip. Eiffel, scenting food, ran across the autobahn, hot in pursuit of the shadow. But the shadow—rabbit, squirrel, hamster, or whatever it may have been—got away. After a few minutes of pointless chase Eiffel reapppeared, his tongue hanging out and his head disappointedly down. A last look, a longing sniff and he started trotting back across the autobahn.

It was all over in a few seconds. At the same moment Lili Marlene heard the high singing sound of the jeep's tires on the concrete surface of the road, the little dog hesitated, and

nfused and frightened, made a run for his mistress and was
caught under the wheels of the racing jeep. The scream of
the brakes mingled with the pitiful yelps of the dog. Lili Marlene dashed out to the jeep. An American MP sergeant was
climbing out, his roundish, rough-looking face expressive of
bewilderment and above all of helpless regret. Hysterical with
grief and rage, Lili Marlene bent over the dog, but it was too

late to do anything for him. She upbraided the sergeant
fiercely in a mixture of Bavarian German and school English.
He stood there helplessly, genuinely sorry for his recklessness,
anxious to do something for the grieved girl. When she began
sobbing he put his arm awkwardly around her shoulders, and
she became calmer.

Together they buried Eiffel beside the autobahn. The
American stood there beside the jeep, brushing the dirt off his
hands. "And now—where to, Fräulein?" he asked, his small
dark eyes twinkling with friendliness.

"I'm going home."

"And where is that?"

"Almfurt, in Bavaria."

"Miss, the whole United States Army is between you and

Bavaria. You'll never make it. Where did you come from?

"Berlin. I got out when the Russians came."

"Look," he said, putting his hand on her arm. "The city is safe now. American and British units are there. You'd better come back with me." His hand tightened persuasively, though not commandingly.

It was clear that he meant well: his actions were formed and shaped by the press of circumstances.

She saw that he was acting in good faith, though she could not suppress a last glimmer of resistance. "Are you telling me that I've *got* to go back to Berlin?" She disengaged her arm from his hand.

"It's for your own good, Fräulein," he said, shrugging his shoulders. His lips formed into a little wry smile. "Yes, you'd better come along back. I'll see that you will be all right." Whereupon he helped her into the jeep, put her overnight case in after her and took off toward Berlin.

By the time they arrived in Berlin, Lili Marlene had decided that Bill Hadley was not at all a bad fellow. He was kind and friendly, and when he offered to get her a place to live in the American Sector, she decided that would be better than trying to re-establish herself in her old apartment which by now might even be bombed or burned out. He ensconced her in a small apartment on Argentinische Allee, after dispossessing two frowzy girls who had been living there with a couple of Red Army soldiers, before the latter had been withdrawn to their own sector. The girls went down the street lugging their belongings, including a supply of vodka, a pair of Russian shoulder boards and other trivialities. One of them shook her fist at Hadley and shouted, "The Bolsheviks will hang you one day."

Hadley turned the apartment over to Lili Marlene and took his leave, but promised to return after he had reported in at his headquarters. A short while later he came back, his arms loaded with packages of food. He dumped the packages in the

.tle kitchen, but he didn't see Lili Marlene. He called her,
vent from front to back looking for her. He turned the handle
of the bathroom door. There she sat, up to her shoulders in a
tub of hot, soapy water, thoroughly enjoying a long-missed
pleasure, her white breasts bobbing up and their points wink-
ing out of the water. Upon seeing him, she gave a little squeal
of surprise, crossed her arms over her exposed bosom. "I
thought the door was locked," she gasped.

His rough-looking face broke into an embarrassed smile.
"Sorry . . ." he apologized. "I—I brought some food and
things." He closed the door and went into the living room.

They had a wonderful meal together, and she began to like
Bill Hadley very much. That night he took her to the Club
Royal. There one could get a thick, black-market steak, have
a choice of liquor and fancy drinks and enjoy good music.
They drank and danced and Lili Marlene almost—almost—
forgot the hopelessness of her situation.

During the course of the evening, an important-looking
civilian came over to their table and asked Lili Marlene to
dance with him. He was Percy Watson, a political aide to the
general, a tall, clean-cut, handsome man of about thirty. He
was an excellent dancer, she discovered, but she did not like
his arrogant and snobbish attitude, his bearing of self-impor-
tance. He bluntly suggested that it would be to her advantage
to "be nice to him." She remained unimpressed, and was glad
to be back sitting with the quiet, unassuming, if not handsome,
Bill Hadley.

It was very late when Hadley brought her home. He took
her up the stairs, came in the apartment with her. Then he
casually took off his blouse and proceeded to make himself at
home. Lili Marlene gave him a negative sign, smilingly held
his coat for him, kissed him lightly and ushered him out into
the hallway. He started to go away and then, remembering
himself like a comedian in a double-take, pounded on the
door. She opened it. With a disarming smile, he told her he

had left the keys to his jeep inside. She went back to look for them, and when she turned round she was in his arms. She felt like laughing at his fumbling but insistent effort. She escaped him, he tried again, caught her, kissed her, they laughed, she freed herself. This laugh-and-play sport went on for some minutes, until finally it became clear to him that he wasn't actually getting any place. "OK, Lili Marlene," he said, out of breath. "You win. Let's have one drink and I'll go quietly."

Neither of them could have said when or why they poured the second drink, the third, and certainly not those thereafter. She was somehow delighted with her new-found friend: this rough-surfaced but gentle American sergeant was like a breath of fresh air blown into her life. Certainly he wanted to sleep with her, like the others, but he was open and honest about it in a naive sort of way. And he would never force her: this she knew and that is why she sat there, alone in her apartment with him, getting tipsy. She felt *en rapport* with Bill Hadley. They talked and laughed and drank. She thought of Eckert and of Sethe; and of Percy Watson with his cold, overconfident manner; and of Karl and of Paul—and then her eyes came to rest on Bill Hadley. She smiled a kindly, genuinely warm smile for him, rose to her feet, intending to take him to the door and say goodnight. Her legs did not obey her commands. She swayed and sank back onto the couch, giggling a little. Then she felt his arms going around her, lifting her: she was being carried: she was placed gently on the bed: she opened her eyes and saw his face. His dark eyes were warm and asking. She closed her eyes and let herself drift into a delicious vagueness.

For a long time there was a vast quietness over the room, then the low rustling, silken sounds of two people completely lost in each other. Not the slightest breeze came to disturb the flimsy curtains of the windows. Outside, a soft white cloud sailed discreetly past a big, yellow, smiling moon. After a long intimate interval, the moon faded and waned and a tiny breeze sprang up to stir the drapes. A bar of light came out of the east and reached into the room: it fell on the painting of an angry stallion, reared and flailing his forefeet: then it sought out a Rubens type nude woman reclining on a red ottoman: it brightened over an ashtray filled with burned-out cigarette stubs near Lili Marlene's bed: shone brightly on her overnight case, opened on a chair, in which had been her treasured silk underthings. The morning's fingers touched her eyelids and she awakened, gently, peacefully, with a look of bright contentment on her face. A bird sang outside, and she closed her eyes briefly, remembering once, long ago, when she had watched with immature understanding a *Zaunkönig* stealing the nectar from a morning-glory. She saw again, but now with a delicious understanding, the tiny bird hovering lovingly over the pink petals of the flower, caressing them with his firm little bill until they seemed to spread and reach out, asking him to come in and take the precious nectar deep in its pistil. The bird's neck stretched, sleek and firm, and its head went in, snuggled for a long time. It came out: went in again: again: again: again: in and out: in and out: deeply, sweetly. Finally it plunged down deep into the flower's body, nestled there for a long moment, ravaging the delicious immature fruit therein. Then it flew away.

Lili Marlene stretched luxuriously. She sat up and the covers slipped from her shoulders. She pulled them back, the air was cold on her naked body. After a while she flung off the covers, slipped out of bed, and, before going into the bathroom, reached underneath the bed and retrieved her silken Parisian panties, where they had been tossed by the rough yet gentle hand of Bill Hadley, long before the *Zaunkönig* had cried out at her window.

This was another day, and she had to survive it—somehow.

That evening there came a knock at Lili Marlene's door. It would be Bill Hadley, and she was glad. All day she had expected him to come. There was a warm, expansive feeling inside her as she opened the door. Instead of Hadley, there stood the immaculate Percy Watson. He smiled. "May I come in?"

"I was expecting Sergeant Hadley," she said disappointedly.

"Yes, I know. I came to tell you that he has been transferred out of Berlin."

"And you had nothing to do with it, I suppose?" she said coolly.

"Oh, I wouldn't say 'nothing,' my dear. You see, it was in line of duty. A first-rate MP was needed in Helmstedt and so I dropped a hint to the right people, and ho! Bill Hadley was just the man. Anyway, Fräulein, it needn't inconvenience you in the slightest. I am here to step right into the breach." He made a little bow and gave a little suave smile.

"Don't bother!" she said angrily.

"But, Fräulein, surely you wouldn't refuse to go out with me! I can take you to places where Sergeant Hadley couldn't get his big foot in."

"No, thanks!"

"I see," he smiled. "But I won't give up. I'll be back. You'll change your mind."

He did come back, every day; sometimes he stopped in twice a day. But Lili Marlene did not change her mind. Finally, however, more to get rid of him than anything else, she told herself, she agreed to go to dinner with him.

He took her to the American Press Club, where requisitioned waiters served American food and liquors on requisitioned china and a requisitioned orchestra played while Americans and their Fräuleins danced on the hardwood floor of the spacious requisitioned dwelling. It proved to be a short and unhappy affair for Percy Watson, for here she met Art Jourdan. A worldly-wise-correspondent of about forty, Art Jourdan was kindly, soft-spoken and sympathetic. They danced together and he took her to the bar.

"Aren't you afraid of Percy Watson?" she asked, remembering what he had done to Sergeant Hadley.

Jourdan smiled. "That guy has power around here all right. But not over correspondents. I brought you over here to find out what you are like. I like you. Maybe you'll come to like me. I think maybe I'd like to make you my girl."

She liked his bold, straight approach. There was a challenging frankness and wholesomeness about it. It was something completely new to her, never experienced before. Others had gone after her with either direct masculine drive or by subtle and ofttimes crude subterfuge. Here was a man who used neither of these offensive methods. And she liked the man: he seemed solid, genuine. She gave him her address.

Art Jourdan and Lili Marlene became good friends. He displayed all the signs of being in love with her. Yet he made no demands upon her. He took her with him everywhere: to cocktail parties, to clubs, mess halls, they were seen together constantly at the Press Club. In his work he traveled extensively. He was always returning from Paris, Vienna, Brussels, London and other great cities with dresses, lingerie, shoes, perfumes and other gifts for her. With all the finery he showered upon her, she became the toast of the American Sector. Although there had as yet been no real romance or intimacy between them, she was considered to be "Jourdan's Fräulein," and everybody kept hands off. But the vain and pretentious Percy Watson kept trying. He was always turning up at her apartment whenever Jourdan was out of town, smiling his half smile, half leer and offering his "help" and asking to take her out. She was polite but firm in her consistent refusal of his solicitude.

Lili Marlene liked Art Jourdan immensely. He was considerate, intelligent, kind. Like most newspapermen, he maintained a youthful attitude toward all things and an extraordinarily keen interest in people. From him she had gained much: she had acquired a vast amount of knowledge, a confident and mature poise, a certain polish, and above all a great tolerance of people and a wise and deep sense of humanity One night, after a wonderful evening of dining and dancing together, when she had looked at him with intense and shining eyes, he took her hands gently in his and said, "Let's go home, Lili Marlene."

She understood, and without hesitation said, "All right Art."

Next morning, when they awakened in her apartment, he told her, in his soft, kindly voice, "Lili Marlene, you probably wonder why I waited so long. Well, I'll tell you. For years I've traveled, covering three-quarters of the globe. I've met all kinds of people, good and bad, great and small. I've done a lot of things: had a lot of fun, a lot of grief: had a few heartaches, perhaps caused a few. Through it all I've learned, above all else, to bear a great respect for the dignity of mankind. Sure, I've wanted to sleep with you from the very first time I saw you. But I couldn't do it until I was sure that you wanted me, too. To take you before you wanted me as I wanted you would have been a crime against your dignity, as well as my own."

She did not speak. Tears flooded her eyes and when she flung herself in his arms they were streaming down her cheeks. "Oh, Art!" she cried in a choked voice.

The love affair with Art Jourdan was wonderful: it seemed mature: it was directionless. He took her with him on trips. She saw Munich, Stuttgart, Frankfurt, Vienna, Paris. She met important people: writers, journalists, businessmen, diplomats. One day, when he was away alone on an extended trip, she received a long letter from him. It came from Cairo, and ended: "Darling, from here I must return to America for a new assignment. It may be that I won't come back to Europe. If I don't I will be sorry. If I do I will, of course, come to you at once. But should we never see each other again, remember

what I have always told you: all things must end. And when
an era or an experience is finished, my dear, don't brood or
grieve or try to recall it. And above all, don't remember the
bitter part of it, but try to remember only the sweet, the
kindly, the good. And you will become richer and more lovely
for having experienced it." She never heard from him again.

Civilian experts and technicians in all fields of the occupation were streaming into Berlin. These were men with freedom, lots of money and big American automobiles. One day,
as Lili Marlene was walking down Argentinische Allee, Dick
Swaggerlee picked her up in his yellow convertible Buick.
Dick Swaggerlee was from Los Angeles. He lived in the heart
of the old city, near Westlake Park, but he told everybody he
was from Hollywood: his yellow convertible convinced the
naive and impressionable. He never directly stated it, but he
endeavored to give the impression that he had been connected
with motion pictures in Hollywood. Actually he had never
seen the inside of a movie studio. He had been the manager
of a chain gasoline station on Wilshire Boulevard and once in
a while some of the movie stars would stop in to fill up with
gas. That's the closest he ever came to the movies. He had
risen from private to captain in the Army Transportation
Corps, and when the war ended, went to Washington and in
the course of the wholesale hiring of bodies to fill the bureau-
cratic slots, he got the job as Liquid Fuel Chief for the US
Sector of Berlin. Lili Marlene had been at loose ends since
Art Jourdan's letter, and the day Dick Swaggerlee came along
she light-heartedly took a chance and climbed in the yellow
convertible.

Swaggerlee at once turned on his charm and began to flatter
her with his usual line. "Baby, you ought to be in pictures
. . . A friend of mine—wonderful guy—ought to be hitting
Berlin this fall. He's a pal of mine. I think I'll . . . yes, I will!
. . . Baby, when this pal of mine from Hollywood gets here,

I'll fix you up with him. Yes, sir, I will do that little favor for you . . ." Lili Marlene was not taken in by Swaggerlee. But she liked him in a wise, reserved sort of way. He was good-looking, dressed handsomely. He was generous and he took her everyplace—and in the beginning, at least, treated her with attentiveness and a certain tenderness.

Dick Swaggerlee came to love Lili Marlene as much as his conceit would allow, and made half-hearted promises to marry her and take her back to Hollywood with him. When drunk he would become very passionate and tell her that she was more beautiful, more photogenic, than the loveliest movie stars. Sometimes his frustration and sense of inferiority would get the better of him and he would become abusive, pound the table or beat his chest and shout what a great fellow he really was and how stupid and small everybody else was. She learned to ignore him in these drunken moods, because she knew that the next day he would be remorseful and repentant. He was a camera enthusiast, and never tired of making pictures of her. He was continually trading cigarettes and coffee for cameras and equipment, and had built a small laboratory in his apartment where he developed and processed his own films.

One Sunday afternoon, when they were driving back from an outing at Wannsee Lake listening to the car radio, the music stopped and a woman's voice came on, giving a political commentary. Lili Marlene was dumbfounded: it was Eva! Delighted and excited to learn that she was still alive, Lili Marlene asked Swaggerlee to drive her over to the radio station.

When they got there, the receptionist told them that Eva had left a few minutes earlier. "She left with Herr Spindler," the girl said.

"Gerhard Spindler?" Lili Marlene asked.

"Yes," the receptionist replied. "They come here together constantly."

Lili Marlene wrote her name and address on a card and handed it to the girl. "Please give this to her."

She never heard from Eva—until the day Percy Watson confronted her with this tell-tale card in her own handwriting. The day he charged her with murder.

Lili Marlene was sitting by the fireplace in the Colony Club, an American officers' and civilians' club, waiting for Dick Swaggerlee who was engaged in a big dice game in the ping-pong room. It was late and she was bored and wanted to go home. From a darkened corner nearby a thick voice growled, "You a Fräulein?"

She turned to see the red glow of a cigar and then the outlines of a smallish man with broad shoulders and a large head slumped in an armchair. As the cigar glowed, she saw that he had prominent features: a large, flared nose, high cheek bones and a stubborn chin. His skin was dark and his eyes were large and brown and had a fierce cast about them, though now clouded with alcohol. "I'm a German girl," she countered.

The cigar bobbed. "Well, it's not your fault you're here, I suppose. Some stupid American brought you here, no doubt. Good word—stupid. *Stupid* American. *Stupid* occupation. Me? I'm stupid, too, I guess. One of the Americans of this big wonderful stupid occupation! The whole mixed-up, erratic, infernal business is stupid! Goddamn stupid!"

She held him boldly with her eyes. "What's wrong with being a Fräulein?" she demanded.

"No moral sense! No moral sense! That's what's wrong!" he shouted as if in a courtroom.

Lili Marlene rose indignantly. He uncrossed his legs, leaned forward and stayed her with a friendly hand. The wild look had left his eyes. "Forgive me, Miss. Nothing personal. It—it's the occupation, I guess. I often rant like this. I didn't mean to offend you. What I said was really aimed at the Americans who behave badly over here. I'm Hermann Gould, the legal advisor for the Americans. I get them divorced, get them married, keep them out of jail, cover up their black-marketing, make official excuses for their general lousy conduct. I suppose I'm just fed up. I'm disgusted. Here, have a cigarette." He opened his silver cigarette case, held it out to her. *"Ober!"* he shouted. When the waiter appeared, he said, "Bring us a drink. Make mine a double bourbon." To her, "You will have a drink with me?"

Thus Lili Marlene made a new friend. She was growing tired of Dick Swaggerlee's drinking and gambling, and especially of his attitude toward her: he made her feel as if she were his private property, something to pick up and put down at his own personal pleasure. So whenever Hermann Gould asked her for a date she was glad to see him. She was fascinated by this fiery and brilliant lawyer. It gave her a deep sense of satisfaction to listen while he shouted denunciation of his fellow Americans. It was good to hear somebody voice the things about the Occupation Forces that she could not.

Hermann Gould was an idealist whose shining towers were battered by man's apparent desire to bring wholesale destruction of civilisation. War had fostered in him a deep sense of guilt for himself and all mankind, and man's lust for war had shocked and unbalanced his delicate spirit. His was the tragedy of a man who could not make up his mind whether to accept the postwar world for what it brutally was, or to beat his brains out hopelessly against its unyielding and defiant bastions. Outwardly he strove to become a cynic, but his deep-rooted kindly nature fought with him. His deep and sincere love for his fellow men was too strong. He was a lost soul.

Hermann Gould loved Lili Marlene, but not like the others. He loved her in a shy and painful way, as if he were afraid to admit it, even to himself. She felt deeply for Hermann Gould, he made her soft and tender inside. There was something indefinable between them, a vague, unreasoning longing which they alike shared. Perhaps it was that they both were in pursuit of the same thing, a vague hope for happiness and peace of soul and mind. Gould, bedeviled by the conflict raging within himself, and Lili Marlene, a victim of the shattered world around her, were drawn day by day inexorably toward each other.

Lili Marlene saw more and more of Hermann Gould and consequently less of Dick Swaggerlee. One night, stewing in his jealously and trying to drown his hurt vanity with excessive drinking, Swaggerlee came to her apartment and accused her of being the "Fräulein of that goddamn Gould." Shaken and humiliated at this accusation, Lili Marlene ordered him out. He was in an ugly, drunken mood, and refused to go. "I'm staying right here," he announced, and took off his coat, his tie, and proceeded to unlace his shoes.

"All right," she said, coolly, "if you won't go, I'll leave."

She got her coat and started out. But he dragged her back. She fought him and he lost control of himself and cuffed her until her face was blue and her eyes blood-shot. When finally she managed to get away she ran down the stairs and went to Hermann Gould's apartment.

Gould was very mellow and sympathetic—and sane—that night. They had a long talk, in which he told her all about himself. He had been raised in an orphanage, educated himself the hard way, got his degree at the University of Chicago, and had begun what promised to be a brilliant career in a reputable La Salle Street law firm when the war came. He told her about Chicago and his friends. As he talked she saw the bitterness in the man; dimly she comprehended that his disillusionment was destroying him. Finally that night, standing with one arm resting on the stained marble mantelpiece and without looking at her, he said simply, "Lili Marlene, if you will marry me I will take you back to Chicago. You can be happy there with me—if you try."

This was, she had long thought, what she wanted: a passport out of the ruins of Germany. But now that it was offered, honestly and with absolutely no strings, her whole being rejected it. It was as if the Imp of the Perverse, abiding on the blood of emotions, was performing and directing her. But it was more than just that. Something in her, something that respected and admired the idealism of this bitter little man, cried out at the same time: "Why don't you fight for your ideals—or bury them? All other men do one thing or the other!" Perhaps it was a German thoroughness in her that made her want to pound against his chest with her fists and compel him to make a decision. And perhaps it was something German in her, too, that made her reject his offer, which she knew was so well-meant. Was she not Lili Marlene, a native of Bavaria, a girl of German stock? What had she to do with the sooty towers of Chicago, the alien murmur of a distant land? Karl would never come back, and neither would Paul. But the good side of the things they had meant to her was there, was in the air she breathed and the houses she knew. She clenched her teeth and drew a long shadowy breath. Crying silently, she picked up her things. "I can't marry you, Hermann Gould," she told him and left.

Next morning Lili Marlene had reached an important decision. She would cut out from these tawdry people. Berlin was getting back on its feet. Marshall money had been poured into the city coffers, building and trade had revived, commerce was going along at a lively pace. It was a large city. She would go to some other district, away from the Americans, and re-establish herself. She would get a job.

She was in the middle of packing, when the door opened and Percy Watson walked in. He stood there, pursing his lips and rocking slightly on the balls of his feet. "Leaving, eh?" he said, with a cat-that-swallowed-the-canary look on his face.

"Figure it out yourself," she said curtly.

"Fed up, huh?"

"I certainly am!" she retorted.

"Is that why you killed him?"

She stopped, frozen, with one hand on the lid of a suitcase. The tone of Watson's voice told her that he was not making a joke. "What are you talking about?"

"Hermann Gould. He was found dead this morning in his billet, with a service .45 beside his body."

"You don't think that I—" She advanced angrily toward him.

"I know what happened. You and Swaggerlee had a fight over Gould last night. You went to Gould's apartment. You left late. This morning he was found dead. I come here and find you packing . . ."

"Dick Swaggerlee didn't do it! He can be pretty nasty. Oh, I know that well enough. But he's not a man who would commit murder."

Watson placed his hands on her shoulders. "Look, Lili Marlene. We know how Gould died. The authorities have pronounced it suicide. *I* could reopen the case. It *could* look bad for you. But I'm your friend, Lili Marlene. I've always liked you. You just forget that we got off to a bad start and we'll let Gould remain a suicide. I'll get you a really nice place to live." He looked disdainfully about him. "This place is a dump, really. You won't come off badly by being my Fräulein."

She flung his hands from her. "Look here, Watson. You do what you think you can to me. But never, never will I be seen even walking down the street with you. You're a vain, conceited ass! Now get out of here and leave me alone! I'm through with men—all of you!"

He stood there, smiling a little silly smile. "I suppose you're going to be a good little girl and go out and get yourself a job?"

"And what's wrong with that?"

"Nothing. Only it's quite impossible for you. You see, we found this in the purse of a person suspected of complicity in espionage against the Allies." He held up the card on which she had written her name and address for Eva. "We arrested a Gerhard Spindler. He's a spy. We picked up a woman he was living with. This was in her purse. Naturally, this card will go into your *Fragebogen*. Who would give you a job? Not the Americans. Not the British. Not the French. No German would dare. So, that leaves you one choice—the Russians . . . But my offer still stands. Think it over. You know where to find me." He turned and walked out.

She got a room in the British Sector. There was, she well knew, no hope of getting a job with any of the Allies. But she did try all the German agencies. Then she went from office to office, from store to store. Sometimes she filled out applications and questionnaires, was told to come back after the customary check was made, but upon returning would be coldly sent away. This went on and on, until she gave up in despair. The haunting thought of Percy Watson's threat and offer did not drive her to him. It hardened and crystallized her determination to remain away from all her old acquaintances, no matter what happened. Down and down her spirits sank, as it became clear that she would not find a job.

Many Germans were tasting prosperity now. They were acquiring automobiles and other luxuries, looking for the good life once again. They had money to spend on girls. Lili Marlene would stand by the window in her apartment at night looking down on Kurfürstendamm, watching the girls loitering there under the lamps. Those girls, too, had somehow come to the end of the pavement; many of them through the same paths of war she had traveled, where there was no Karl or Paul. What had her resolution been worth, she wondered bitterly. How long could she hold out, and she contemplated the few marks that remained in her purse.

Then the letter came. It was from Karl's father, in Almfurt. It had followed her by a circuitous route from address to address, and when it finally reached her it was covered with stampings. The letter said that Karl was not dead but had been a prisoner in a camp in Russia. He was, at long last, being released. Karl's father urged her to come back home. She looked at the date of the letter. Karl had been home for weeks now. She felt a constriction of heart and an empty cold feeling ran all through her: she should have been there to greet him when he stepped off the train: a wave of nostalgia swept through her: tears came to her eyes as she thought of Karl and of her old home town. The years between then became blurred and unimportant in her mind. She sent Karl a telegram, telling him she was coming home.

The clock in the Almfurt church tower above Lili Marlene struck eight, bringing her out of her reminiscence and back to her present situation. In a few minutes now she would see Karl. There would be a reunion. Later in the presence of his family and friends they would be married. And then—later, at just the right time—she would tell him of her life in those years between. He would brood about it for a time. But she would lavish her most delicate attentions on her husband, coax and fondle him, and so enamor him that he would soon forgive her for her past. She would strive with all her endeavor to be a good wife. In time it would cease to bother him. And the nightmare of the ten, eleven, twelve years since his departure would be wiped out, erased, made clean again as if at the touch of a merciful ministering angel. She would be the woman she had started out to be when she was a little pig-tailed girl in the schoolroom, the woman she had never ceased to be, really, from the time Karl's outstretched fingers had lightly, despairingly, promisingly touched hers as the train pulled out of the little railway station of Almfurt.

She rose from the stone bench, crossed the street to the sidewalk, and started walking toward the railway station. When she passed Kutscher's Restaurant, the night manager was standing by the door, impatiently awaiting his relief. "Well, Peaches-and-cream, what about it?" he said to Lili

Marlene. "There she is." He indicated the convertible parked across the street by the church. "We'll gas her up and take off, baby. You just say the word."

She held her head straight ahead and gave no sign that she even heard him.

Lili Marlene approached the station cautiously. She didn't want to see Karl too suddenly. She began to tremble a little. What would he be like, after all those years? Certainly, he would be thinking similar thoughts about her. And what was she like, really? Well, she'd tell him. It was good that she could tell him herself, and choose her own time for it. He'd understand. After all, there was hardly a life that was not, in some degree, touched by the same sadness that stood between her and Karl. Yes, she was sure he would understand, and forgive. No, Karl would not, could not, censure her. The faces of the men she had known whirled before her confusedly: Corporal Paul Halder, Sethe, Hadley, Jourdan, Swaggerlee, Gould. And she chased them all away—and there was Karl . . . Karl, big Karl, fair-faced, soft-mannered Karl, the boy, the youth, the man she had loved: would love again. As the distance between her and the station fell away, she became calm.

She stepped bravely up to the platform. The train had already pulled out. And there was Karl. She saw him only in profile. He was the same Karl, only older, sadder and wiser-looking. He was standing between his father and *Eva!* She froze in her tracks. The situation was incandescently clear in her mind. Eva had always wanted Karl. Oh, she was the clever one, all right. She had talked her way out of whatever trouble she might have been involved in with Gerhard Spindler, rushed back to Almfurt as soon as she got word of Karl's release. By now she had spread the ill-tidings about Lili Marlene. Eva had, in the end, won. As a husband Karl Ingolmann would live steadily and provide well. He would one day come into his father's immense lands and would become a man prominent among all the *Bürgers,* a man of substance, of high honor. And all this would be Eva's. Lili Marlene saw Karl's mother—she had always been the understanding and sympathetic one—standing in the background, looking anxiously through the crowd of disembarked passengers for her. She wanted to run to the kindly woman and cry out all.

Instead she turned quickly, ran out of the station, ran across the street, over the little bridge, tears streaming down her cheeks. She hoped the night manager would still be at Kutscher's. She craved to be instantly back in Berlin, to enter the only life left for her there. She was hopelessly defeated now, and she yielded as a drowning man might yield after the actual sting of death had gone from his lungs, or as a tired and aged saint might yield up his spirit to the Unknown. Fate had chased and chastised her until she, too, had at long last, come to the end of the pavement.

The red-headed night manager of Kutscher's drew the convertible up to the curb in front of Lili Marlene's apartment house, got out, took her handbag, and went up the stairs with her, a look of lust and triumph on his face. At the door she took her bag out of his hand, gave him a pleading, negative look. "But see here, Peaches-and-cream, I've gone to a good deal of bother for you. It's a long way from Almfurt to Berlin, and"—he snickered—"I didn't come here just to sightsee."

"Not now," she said.

Consternation and anger clouded the redhead's face. Then, sensing the girl's resoluteness, he forced a little smile. "I understand, Peaches-and-cream," he said, trying to affect a bigness of attitude and not show that he was afraid to challenge her determination. "You must be tired out. It was a long hard drive. All day yesterday and all last night without a let-up. My *Opel* can't make plane time, you know. Tell you what you do. You get some rest. I'll go out and put the car away, might even catch a few hours shut-eye myself." He snickered. "Hope

I don't oversleep. Anyway, I'll give you plenty of time, Peaches-and-cream. You'll find me a right pal. We're going to get along just fine—just fine." He pulled her to him, kissed her unresponding lips, and went down the stairs.

That night Lili Marlene stood by the window in her room, looking out on the scene below her. A fine mist was swirling down, causing the pavements to glisten with hue of steel, blue and yellow in the funnel-like glows of the street lamps. Girls were already on their beats. Some were walking slowly up and down, swinging their large purses casually, others were loitering boredly under the lamps. Lili Marlene stood there, purse in one hand, furled umbrella in the other, prepared to go out and take her place among them. But she hesitated, dreading this initial momentous step, hating the ordeal, loathing to venture forth to join, once and for always, that sorority of lost girls down there below her.

While she stood there, gazing down at Kurfürstendamm, a startlingly familiar figure came into the scene. She caught her breath. Could it be! Could it possibly be him? She moved closer to the window, strained her eyes to see through the dull, wet night. His face lifted toward her window. It *was* Karl! Karl—looking for her! Then she saw something that she had not seen at the station in Almfurt. He was an amputee. One leg was missing.

She ran out of the room, down the stairs, and toward him. He saw her coming and tried to run to her. In his excitement he lost his crutch and fell to the pavement. "Karl! Karl!" she cried. "You came for me! You need me."

He looked up at her and she saw in his eyes all the tenderness and understanding a man can hold for one he loves above and beyond all else in this world. "Need you, *mein Liebling?*" he said gently. "Yes, Lili Marlene. But I love you. And I want you. I'll always love you and want you."

THE END

THE PRICE OF WAR

A JEEP STANDS a little distance off the turnpike, half concealed by the overhanging branches of linden trees. It is late afternoon and the sun, large and blood-red, seems immobile in the midst of space, unable to drop down behind the dark hills. It hangs there, astonished and grieved by the scene under the linden tree.

A soldier is lying on his back in the grass, one leg drawn up under his body, his arms flung limply. His white face is turned toward the sun, whose slanting rays glint against the still half-closed eyes. Beside the soldier sits a young girl, her slender hands around the handle of a knife that is thrust to its hilt in the soldier's neck. Her face, too, is toward the blood-red sun. It is a beautiful face, with high cheeks, firm straight nose and large Prussian-blue eyes. Her hands close around the bone handle of the knife so tightly that the knuckles visibly whiten. She draws the blade out of the soldier's neck and flings it away in the grass. A rill of blood follows, running sinuously down into the shirt. Her lips quiver and her hands go to her face, covering her eyes. *I will not cry. I must not. He had to die. I've known it all along. But why, why? WHY!* She leans over and kisses the dead soldier lightly on the lips, her honey-yellow hair caressing his still face, and the answer comes incandescently clear in her mind. *I shouldn't have loved him.*

A great butterfly describing a huge arc in the field flashes golden in the sunlight. Her eyes follow its fluttering until it becomes lost in dancing flight. Her thoughts soar on and beyond the butterfly, back, back as far as she can remember . . .

Gretl's mother pulled a sweater over the child's head, art-fully propelling little arms through the tight sleeves until tiny fists popped out. But Gretl was unmindful. She was watching a yellow and black butterfly as it soared from flower to flower in the yard. "There now. Mother's girl is ready to go and meet Daddy."

Tiny feet pattered down the path and she was swept up in mighty arms, tossed high, enfolded and kissed. Riding back to the house on Daddy's shoulders she remembered her butterfly. But it was gone, not to be seen among the flowers in the field beyond. There were, though, earth-colored birds flying home-ward, sweeping close to the friendly land, for the day was done. Somewhere from the shelter of the grass a cricket cried to its mate in a plaintive, metallic voice. In the distance a large, black bird, wings spread, was circling ominously over a dead beech tree, whose gaunt limbs were raised to the sky like arms. The uncouth bird and the black arms of the tree brought to the child's mind thoughts of the evil witch in fairy tales. Instinctively she clung to her Daddy and covered her face with her tiny hands. When they got to the house she heard him tell her mother that he was going away. She heard her mother's shocked voice: "Spain?" And she heard Daddy say proudly: "Legion Condor!"

Little Gretl was sad and bewildered, unable to understand. A heavy hushed atmosphere pervaded all the rooms through-out, and the house was filled with people who moved quietly and solemnly about. Her mother, with sad, damp eyes, had told her and her brother Adolf that Daddy had gone away— to the angels—and would not return. Adolf said, "Yes, Mother, I understand, and I am proud of Father. I will become a soldier, too." But Gretl could not understand. She was lonely and confused and afraid; she wanted to feel her little fist in his big, safe hand.

She went into the room where he was, hesitating on the

threshold. Some men and women were sitting about, respectfully silent and grave-looking. Adolf was sitting bravely with the men. They all regarded her sorrowfully. One of the women burst into muffled sobs: "Poor child! Poor child!"

She approached the casket, stood on her toes and looked in, and a deep hush fell over the chamber. Could that be Daddy? She remembered him as a big, lively, smiling man. He was so still! And he was not smiling. The powder on his face, intending to conceal its wan pallor, was smeared around his mouth, making it appear twisted. She had an inclination to wipe it off but checked herself, not knowing why. The air, drenched with the pungent perfume of the flowers banking the casket, was a lethargic complement to the purple of his eyelids. His hands appeared cold as marble! Those strong, warm hands. The black of the rosary, which was entwined about his pale fingers, stood boldly out against their whiteness, and there was an angelic beauty about their stillness, like the hands of Saint Joseph, in her church. An empty lost feeling came over her, her eyes brimmed with tears, and she ran and climbed on the bed with her mother, who gathered her to her bosom. She could not understand why her Daddy, whom she loved dearly, had to be taken away from her. Nor was she ever to understand why those she came to love dearly would have to die—blown out of her arms and out of this world like drifting leaves.

Five years had passed since Gretl and her mother had come to live at Grandfather's. It was a lovely old place, near the Rhine. It gave the appearance of having been there forever. Its stone-wall house with red roof and its huge barn, garden, fields and orchard, all surrounded by a gray stone fence, seemed indeed incrusted with time. It was springtime and the orchard was in bloom. Gretl lay underneath a queenly apple-tree glowing with delicate pastel color. Her arms were around Dolf, her brown and black Boxer, who beat his tail on the ground and licked her fingers. They were inseparable, each the protector of the other.

A pebble struck her on the cheek. She turned and saw Gerd standing on the flat ridge of the old fence, grinning down at her and Dolf. The Boxer got up and barked his happy approval, and the boy leaped to the ground, dragging after him two cane fishing poles. Gretl was delighted, and presently she, Gerd and Dolf were off toward the stream in the nearby woods.

Gerd took a red, wriggling worm from a tin can, telescoped it on a fish-hook, handed the pole to Gretl. She went to a high place on the bank, sat down, crossed her legs, and dropped the baited hook in the water, determined to make the first catch. In a few minutes the cork bobbed and she flung her fish out of the stream. Dolf pranced with delight, ventured his sniffling nose to the floundering creature but withdrew in disgust. Gerd rebaited Gretl's hook and she stuck the sharpened butt of the pole in the bank, suspending the line over the water, and lay back on the grassy crest and watched the clouds sailing by. She loved to daydream.

Daddy used to tell her that the clouds were the coffins of those who had died being rolled into heaven. It was nice to think of them that way. She wondered which one was Daddy's. She decided on a majestic-looking cumulus and decreed it to be his. Could he look down and know that she was thinking of him? She closed her eyes and remembered his big powerful hands and how wonderful and safe it was in his arms, close to his breast.

Dolf whined. She opened her eyes and saw that her pole was bobbing nervously. She whirled out another fish, which Gerd strung along with the others. As the sun slid down behind a long green ridge they went home, poles slanting on their shoulders, and their thighs touching now and then as they walked along close together. Gerd carried the catch, strung on a cord. Dolf trotted along in front of them, tongue out and tail wagging, occasionally looking back to keep track of them. The evening chill had come, and they were tired and hungry.

And that was about all the childhood Gretl ever knew. One September first buglers awakened the army, and the army awakened the land, and a storm mounted in the skies of Europe, full of evil and foreboding for those who heard it, and began to lay the world in ruins. No more idle hours at the corner ice-cream parlor after school; no more house parties with funpacked games; no football and sports; no silk stockings, high heels, red nails, hayrides, picnics. Hers was a childhood spent in the stirring, tense atmosphere of war where a hierarchy and a nation was in battle for the world: a childhood spent in the Hitler Youth; backing up the soldiers fighting at the front, sewing, training, hiking, attending political lectures: soldiers, shortages, rationing, victories and defeats, blackouts, air-raids, cellars: fleeting hours spent in Gerd's arms, stolen from the grim and evil business of war.

And there were funerals.

Gretl, her mother, and her grandfather went into Wiesbaden to see Gerd and Adolf off to the front. The two boys had enlisted together, taken their training in the same camp. Now they were being shipped out to battle. Gerd had been attached to a unit ordered to the Eastern Front, while her brother Adolf had been drafted into the *Waffen-SS* and was being sent out to the Western Front. The war was old now, and the proud, brave farewells had worn off. There were no longer thoughts of quick victory and glorious marches back to the *Vaterland*. Indeed, farewells were attended with tears and thoughts of death and defeat.

Gretl's mother kissed Gerd tenderly and clung to her son Adolf for a long, long time. Her grandfather shook hands with the boys and put them on the train. Gretl went into the car with Gerd. They held each other close, whispered all the tender things they could think of, kissed each other every moment, made fervent promises. Gretl did not cry, she would not cry—until the train had left. She regretted with all her young heart that they had not been married, in spite of their age, before he had to go away.

Then he was gone and she was standing on the platform, a lonely stillness around her and a desolate, empty feeling inside her. She turned away, trying to fix him in her heart as she had seen him there—his broad shoulders, his brilliant smile, his bright, open face with tufts of sandy hair trying to obscure it.

Since there was no gasoline to spare, grandfather had brought them to the city in the buggy. Gretl and her mother waited in the station while he went to fetch the conveyance. Then the air-raid came. Gretl's mother took her by the hand and ran to the concrete bunker, pushed her down the steps and went back looking for grandfather.

When the planes had dropped their cargo of death and fire and all clear had been sounded, they found her mother's body among the others in the wrecked station. Not far away lay her grandfather, dead beside the smashed buggy and mangled horse.

Gretl was overcome with an exciting, nervous, delicious trepidation. Today Gerd would be home on his first furlough; and, according to their plans made through the exchange of letters, they would be married. It would be a breathless wedding and a breathless honeymoon, before he had to go back to the front, which was hourly receding and contracting as the Russians hammered their way toward the Oder and Berlin and the Allies drove headlong to the Rhine. They wouldn't go away anywhere; they'd have their honeymoon right here, playing and running over the hills and through the woods as they had done in their childhood. They would miss old Dolf, who had been laid to rest in the orchard for three years now, and it was a pity that her brother Adolf could not be with them. Adolf loved her very much, and she him. But Father Gerhard would be there to help with the wedding. He was a life-long friend, kind and considerate. All would go well.

She stepped out of the big white porcelain bath-tub and looked at herself in the full-length mirror which panelled the door. Her ivory glistening body rose with exquisite, firm and delicate contour from the sun-bathed mat on which she stood dripping, like a silver reed uprising from an enchanted pool. Her large blue eyes, beneath masses of hair that resembled new-made honey, were brilliant with happiness. Their lids' golden fringe continually kissed her soft, peach-bloom cheeks with rare excitement. The wild joy in her heart seemed to spill out and sparkle all over her. A warm breeze rippling through the open window brought the scent of flowers. Outside the sun was hot and bright, and the day was one of those that stir the earth, make it alive, break open the seed in order to animate the sleeping bit of life therein, and cleave the bud so that the young leaves may spring forth. A bright blue sky was smiling and all the world seemed joined in a lovely symphony to celebrate Gretl's wedding. But this full, impatient bud was not to be disturbed yet . . .

Gerd did not come that day, nor the next. Then the letter came . . . "We regret to inform you that Private Gerd Koertner has given his life for *Führer* and *Vaterland* . . ."

The war ended with a great foreboding for Gretl. What would happen to her now? All those so close to her, those she loved so much, had been taken by the war. It was as if her love had been a curse upon them. The cessation of killing and suffering was for her like the interim when the clock is about to strike and one hears that little grinding noise as the hammer is raised to strike the bell, breaking in on the peace and quiet of the room. She remained close to the farm, waiting, waiting for something terrible to happen to her. Nothing happened and eventually she grew accustomed to her lonely and seemingly useless existence. Adolf eventually returned, an embittered and disappointed soldier. He regretted that he had gotten into the fighting too late. Germany was not defeated, he claimed. The nation had lost the war, but they had not been beaten—there would come another day.

Then she met Corporal Wheeler—Sonny Wheeler, his friends called him. She was walking down the turnpike near her home one day, when he came along in his jeep and offered her a lift. She withdrew to the side of the road, saying she did not need a ride, ready to run away. But his winning, boyish smile and open face changed her mind, and eventually she let him drive her home to the farm. It was the beginning of a new and wonderful time for Gretl. Sonny, it turned out, had been raised on a farm in Wisconsin; and his life, though he had lived it thousands of miles away, had not been far different from her own. His brother had been killed in the early days of the war and another brother was missing in Korea. Sonny and Gretl discovered they were kindred spirits at once. They spent all of his free hours together. They roamed the fields and woods, went fishing together. And Sonny brought her a dog as an Easter gift, a young shepherd, which she named Wheels (he seemed to be all clumsy legs, and rolled whenever he fell). Theirs was a tender, sweet love, unsullied and pure as clear brook water, as clean as the winds that undulated the grasses in the fields.

So it followed as the night the day that they would marry and Sonny would take her back to his home in Wisconsin. Her life there would continue as it had begun, before it was interrupted by the war, in rustic happiness. All details had been attended to, and a large sheaf of papers had been signed and documented and sealed. Sonny had picked her up in his jeep and they were on their way to see the chaplain in Wiesbaden when Adolf stopped them on the turnpike. Sonny pulled off the road and as he greeted the German boy with a cheery "Hi,

Adolf!" was stabbed in the throat by that embittered former SS soldier.

The butterfly soars out of view and Gretl's eyes catch a great crow circling over a dead tree in the distance. "Caw! Caw! Caw!" it screams. Sailing close, it alights on a fence post, sits there and stares at the girl with ebon, beady eyes. The blood-red sun tiredly gives up and slips down behind the hills, its lingering flames turning the sky into a glow of fire. A soft breeze comes and plays over the dead soldier, touching his soft, unruly hair. The wind comes from the distant Alps, warming its icy fingers as it passes over the hills and plains, and would lose itself beyond the Rhine and the Elbe in the prairies toward Poland and Russia. It passes through Gretl, stroking her heart coolly—coldly. She rises and now, finally, her eyes fill and the tears course down her cheeks. Her finger-nails dig into the palm of her hands. *"Why—why must I pay again and again and again the price of war?"*

She goes to the turnpike, starts walking toward Wiesbaden. She knows what she must do. She must turn her brother Adolf in to the police for the murder of Corporal Sonny Wheeler.

OVERNIGHT PASS

PRIVATE WILLIE MOSS swung his lanky body down from the coach as soon as the train had come to a stop in the high-vaulted, immense and grimy Frankfurt station. He wove his way through the stream of people toward the exit portal, went through the RTO waiting room and stood in line at the currency exchange window. He had twenty-two dollars with which to buy marks. He wouldn't spend it all this night. He'd keep some of it back, in case he got another pass in a few days. He should have at least two girls on that much money.

Willie, a leggy soldier with broad shoulders, long arms and a thin, flat body, moved slowly up to the window where a haughty German clerk made change for the line of soldiers with the superior, disdainful air of one serving persons whom he considered to be far beneath him. Willie looked at his watch. It was five o'clock. He had all night, until six tomorrow morning before he had to be back in barracks at Mannheim.

He crossed the concourse in front of the *Hauptbahnhof*, made his way through the press of people who were entering the station in increasing swarm, and went toward a little beer *Bräustübel* across the street. The faces of the people lingered in his mind. They did not look like city people; they had the faces of the country people and small town people of his native mid-Southern homeland. He reflected how lucky he was to be in the army. When he first received his draft notice he had thought it a great injustice. But he was glad now. The army had opened up a whole new life for him, a life which was far better than the narrow and confined one he had left, across the railroad tracks, down by the brick kiln, back in Jackson. He liked the gray, foreign atmosphere of Germany, the fabulous age-encrusted walls of Gothic time and towers. He fingered the mark notes in his pocket and felt rich and expansive. For Willie, Frankfurt meant nights of joy. He had had good luck in getting girls in Frankfurt.

Inside the *Stübel* he lingered over his beer and thought of the girls he had got when on previous passes. In these memories he felt the tongueless swelling of wild joy. He thought of the blonde he had had last week, of her soft rosy dimpled thighs and firm up-cupped breasts. But when he had got her in bed he discovered that she was not a real blonde. He felt cheated. Later, though, when he was falling asleep with his hot cheek on her white breast, he didn't mind.

He took out his money. There was a purplish fifty-mark note, a green twenty and a faded-blue ten, plus some change. He carefully folded the fifty and slipped it behind his ID card in its little leather case. He'd save this back against the next pass he'd get. He finished his beer, went up the street to the Schumann Snack Bar and had a plate of ham and eggs. When he descended the stairs to the street, the smoky old-gold yellow of the sun was dying over the darkened hills beyond the city. In the street there was the curious loneliness of early evening, a lull and a desertion, an attentive waiting, the pale prelude before the night. It gave Willie a strange and pleasant feeling, presaging for him that intoxicating, sweet and savage, wild and tender thrill of woman—a woman all his own—for brief moments, brief hours; but however brief, it meant a lifetime of exultance and supreme joy for Willie Moss, who could not forget that he came from across the tracks down by the brick kiln.

He went up Taunus Strasse to a bar where he knew girls would be gathering at this time of day. When he entered the place some men were talking at a table near the bar. They paused and looked up at him with the intent, curious stare common to German men interrupted in conversation. He felt their eyes in his back as he went to the bar and climbed on a stool. His manner betrayed a mixture of defiance and diffidence that the occupation soldier feels in the presence of men who he is sure bear a deep resentment, if not actual hatred, for him. He turned and gave them a sharp and casual stare, then ordered a beer.

He drank several steins and all the while people came and went behind him. He turned round on his stool and looked the place over. The men at the table were gone, and in their place were three girls. Two were brunettes and one was a brightly bleached blonde. The brunettes wore dark, drab, rusty-looking clothes, and their faces had sullen, almost heavy casts to them. The blonde's hair was piled high on her head and the wall light behind her made her ears appear too pink and too large. She was wearing a sherry-colored dress cut very low in front, and as she leaned over chatting gaily with her companions the deep V of her bosom showed, curvacious and creamy. Willie squirmed on his stool.

One of the brunettes smiled at him, the one who was not chewing gum, and he noticed that her mouth was red and pleasant, but the gold tooth in front cancelled out her charm. He gave her no sign. His gaze was avidly on the blonde, who, aware that Willie was stripping her naked with his eyes, was studiedly looking through and beyond him, trying hard not to take any notice that she was being noticed. He turned his back to them and ordered another beer; this time he told the bartender to bring him a cognac, too. He tossed off the cognac and sipped his beer.

He had another cognac and beer and decided to give the blonde a second chance. He turned round, and she was smiling toward him. He slipped off the stool, the corners of his mouth going up in a broad smile, which suddenly died on his face. She was not smiling at him but at the three soldiers who had just come in the door and were approaching the girls' table. He saw that the three girls had been waiting for the soldiers. He paid the bartender and went out. He didn't want the oldiers to see that he was trying to pick up one of their girls.

Willie was frustrated and plagued with a lonely feeling. He regretted that he had not gone for the blonde before her friends came in. He had money in his pocket and the pick-up probably would have been successful. Everywhere there was the quiet bustle of an awakening. A new night was beginning in these ancient streets enriched by hundreds of years of adventure and countless people from all corners of the earth. Across the street he saw a pretty Fräulein leading a little boy of about four or five years. The girl was very fair but the child had dusky satin skin and kinky hair. Willie frowned, then he smiled. He found in the sight of this girl and her child a confused, inexplicable joy. The gentle fingers of the cognac began to caress him, his frustration vanished and a mood of defiance and revolt took possession of him. He knew of another place, a fancier place, more expensive. He had never been there but he had heard some of his buddies talk about it in the barracks. There were bound to be prettier girls there, more expensive to be sure, but a better grade of merchandise. Confident now, he walked rapidly toward the place.

The bar was of polished hardwood and the mirror behind it was decorated with colored neon lights. This was indeed fancy. There was a bar-maid, who had bronze-red hair, a rosebud mouth, and the calculating face of a human cash register. The stools had twisted chrome legs and overstuffed leather seats with little chrome rails for back rests. No bar stool for him this time. He selected a table (all the tables were covered with snow-white table cloths) and almost instantly a black-jacketed waiter appeared and bowed discreetly. He was about to order a beer and cognac but thought better of it and instead said, trying to show a casual, familiar air, "A gin fizz, please."

While he waited for his drink he took inventory of the place. Several girls were there, sitting in twos and threes. At a table not far from his, however, sat a girl alone. She was fair

and blonde, not a bleached blonde like the girl he had see
earlier. This one's hair was of a golden hue and it looked
smooth and soft. It was combed back over her head and caught
together with a little blue ribbon, from whence it flowed
shining, freely and profusely. "Peaches 'n cream," Willie
thought, and warmed inside toward her. "She looks good
enough to eat! She's a real blonde, blonde all over."

The waiter brought his gin fizz. He drank it down like it
was beer, ordered another one. Nodding toward the blonde's
table, he added, "And ask the lady what she'll have."

The waiter went to the girl's table, leaned over, spoke
briefly to her. She glanced toward Willie, hesitated, then spoke
with the waiter. When the waiter reappeared, on the tray beside Willie's gin fizz was a tall glass of something pink which
he set down in front of the girl before delivering Willie's
drink. She gave Willie a quick casual look, picked up her
glass and sipped its contents. Willie took his drink and went
over to her table. "I hope you speak English," he said, by way
of opening conversation.

The girl glanced quickly around the room, a furtive, embarrassed expression on her face. Nobody was paying any attention. "Yes, I speak English," she said. "Why did you want
to buy me a drink, soldier?"

"I like you. I sure enough do, that's why."

"Why me? There's lots of other girls here." She looked
straight at him, coolness, defiance on her face.

Willie avoided her large, light blue eyes. She had suddenly
robbed him of his self-assurance, put him ill at ease. "Look
here, Fräulein," he said, determined to find out exactly where
things stood, "you won't be mad if I ask you something right
out, will you? You *are,* well, one of the girls?"

She fumbled in her purse, found a cigarette, stuck it in her
red mouth, leaned a little toward him in a gesture asking for
a light. "So, you like me, soldier?"

Willie smiled broadly, and his teeth shone bright and white. "Lots! What's your name, Fräulein?"

"The boys call me Gaby. You know what I mean, soldier. How much do you like me? How much can you afford?"

"Gabbie. I sure enough like that name."

"It's Gaby, not Gabbie; and I don't talk a lot. How much, soldier, to go with me?"

"Well, last week I had me a girl, a right wonderful girl, but not a real blonde like you. She stayed with me all night, until five in the morning. And she didn't ask for but twenty marks. She'd have stayed longer only I had to get up and ketch the train for Mannheim."

"Twenty marks! Soldier, you'd better go and get her again tonight. I never go for less than forty, and for the whole night you'd have to give me a hundred."

"A hun'ert marks! That's more'n twenty dollars. I never paid more'n twenty marks. And sometimes I get a girl to stay all night with me for that. Besides, I only got twenty marks."

She gave him an impersonal look, blew a little cloud of smoke in his face. "Sorry, soldier."

The finality in her voice told Willie he was being dismissed, as if a door had been abruptly closed in his face. He felt like a bargain-crazed shopper who was about to lose out on a good thing. He wanted this girl, wanted her hard, wanted her savagely and fiercely, with a wild unreasoning urge—now that she had put the price out of reach.

"Look, Gabbie," he said in a husky, urgent voice, "I'll come clean with you. I got more'n twenty marks. But I haven't got a hun'ert. I'll give you forty. That's what you said you wanted. But you've got to stay with me till I have to get up in the morning to ketch my train back to the barracks."

"Sorry, soldier." She had now begun to look bored.

"How 'bout fifty? For a night with you, Gabbie, I'll go the works."

"It's a hundred. And my name's Gab-y—not Gabbie. you can't afford it, soldier, I've got a date in ten minutes, an I don't want him to see me with you."

Willie got up, stung and defeated. He laid a ten mark note on the table for the drinks and left. He went to the bar and tossed off two cognacs, quick and neat. Then he went to the men's room, took out his ID card case and slipped the purple fifty mark note out. He went back to the bar, had another cognac, then went boldly to the blonde's table again.

"You said you'd go for a quick one for forty marks. OK, I got it." He laid the fifty mark note on the table.

"How long you expect for that, soldier?"

"What you said. Just a little while."

"But my date's coming any minute. I can't leave now."

Willie was desperate. The inside of his legs tingled; he ached in his groin. This girl was driving him crazy. "Please, Gabbie! You said you'd go with me for forty marks. I'm giving you fifty. You've *gotta* go with me, Gabbie: Come on please . . ."

She looked at the fifty mark note, glanced quickly around the room, was about to sweep it up when Willie's hand closed over it. "Listen," she said, talking through motionless lips. "You go ahead. I'll meet you outside. I got a room up the street."

"How do I know you'll come?"

"Go ahead! Hurry before my date gets here. I'll be right out."

Willie went outside and waited a little distance up the street, away from the door. "She won't come," he thought. "She just wanted to get rid of me. I should have let her keep the money. She's mad now, real mad. I should have taken a chance with her." Then the door winked open and she was coming toward him.

Willie was overjoyed. There was no longer any resentment in him towards her for not wanting to be seen leaving with him. She was his now, and he would possess her as no man had ever possessed her before. He was completely confident of his superior virility. He would make her cling to him with her heart, her viscera, her bosom and all her passions. She would, as others had done before, cry out with love and rapture in his arms. When they got to her room, he'd not let her turn on the light. He'd take her quickly, and she would forget that he was Willie Moss, a nobody from across the railroad tracks down by the brick kiln of a little Southern town. She would even forget all about the hundred marks, and the fact that he was a Negro.

YANKEE BARGAIN

STEVE HARDSHAW knew he had to die. His captors would give him a slow and terrible death. They had already begun the torture. His right leg was a swollen, watery blister from the white-hot irons, the great toe reduced to a charred cinder by the blazing bamboo slits inserted under the nail. His chest was covered with throbbing red blotches from red hot coins the soldiers had pitched at him as their idea of fun. But even the copper-noduled bludgeon which had rendered his back like a piece of raw beefsteak had not made him talk.

As yet the soldiers had not laid a hand on the others, lashed to a common stake just outside the tent. But Hardshaw knew that they, too, would die slowly and horribly. For the Communists, inspired by their fanatical white-skinned leaders, craved a feast of torture first, to indulge their hate and to strike terror in the hearts of their enemies who would hear of their deed. Hardshaw's broad mouth tightened and he squirmed painfully against his bonds as he thought of what was in store for these loyal little Koreans who had fought superbly and followed him with a gallant one-for-all-all-for-one spirit.

The tent flap was pulled back. Through the opening Hardshaw saw his four battle companions, lashed and sprawled in the black dirt around the steel shaft driven into the ground. Joe, Mike, Solly, Spud—names he had given them because he couldn't pronounce or remember their native ones, affectionate names he had borrowed from some of the gang he had grown up with in his little Texas home town. The *tableau* remained with him long after the Communist captain let the flap fall back in place behind him.

Hardshaw looked up into the oriental captain's bronzed face. His cold gaze met the native's black eyes. Hardshaw was not afraid to die. This he had proved many times. His comrades outside the tent had witnessed his reckless defiance of death repeatedly in the last days while they tried to fight their way back to their own lines. But it was the thought of it all ending this way that he could not bear—and the lingering manner of their death. Unless there was, perhaps, a bargain he could make—with himself as the pawn . . .

"Cut me loose!" His voice was bold, commanding. "I'm ready to talk."

The heavy eyelids slid up. The captain thrust a hand out the entrance of the tent. A soldier came in and cut Hardshaw's bonds. The American stood up, balancing himself on his good foot. "With my knowledge you can win a great victory," he spoke down to the little captain. "You will be decorated in Moscow! You can never force me to talk." He grinned, his grey-blue eyes hardening. "You know that now. But maybe a bargain, Captain—"

The Oriental eyed him with interest. "And your price?"

The tenseness went out of Hardshaw. In a confident voice he gave his terms. He must have one of the captured jeeps, and safe conduct through the Communist lines. "It's a cheap price, Captain," he said, "for the fame and great power my knowledge will bring you."

Hardshaw watched his man. He saw the greedy flash of ambition in the little captain's face. Behind those cruel eyes lay the lust for power, an opportunist's acceptance of stepping stones as he found them. The Texan knew he must not let such a man ponder over a bargain. He whetted the Communist's appetite by raising the ante. "And you must give me $10,000 of the American currency you captured in the raid on our convoy at the Kongju ferry. You see, I know what was in those sealed portfolios."

The captain stopped pacing up and down and was now facing the American with a new respect.

"The jeep and the money must be ready within an hour," Hardshaw continued. "Then I will outline such a victory for you that your name will become a household word in all the Communist world! With my knowledge of position, strength, logistics, this is possible."

The man looked at him as if he were weighing the proposition and seeing things beyond the encampment.

In his final shrug and curt nod, Hardshaw knew he had gotten through to the little oriental captain.

The jeep drew up alongside the tent and Hardshaw, hopping on his good foot, checked it carefully. He made sure the gas tank and radiator were filled, checked the oil. He started the motor, tested the gears, examined all tires, including the spare, and made sure the necessary tools were in the repair kit. Throughout this business he kept his eyes turned away from his companions. Yet he felt their eyes burning into his back even as the red-hot coins had burned into his body. Only once did he glance across at them. In the eyes of all of them was loathing for his treachery. Solly, the expert machine-gunner who had been recommended for decoration, spat into the dust, eyes fierce with contempt.

When the money was brought, to escape the bitter looks of his comrades, Hardshaw slipped into the tent to count it, arrange it in neat packs, and store it in his musette bag, which he strapped securely across his torn and burning shoulders. The Communist captain watched these proceedings with the twist of an amused smile. He was now completely sure of the American. He unrolled a map of the terrain, threw a large notebook on the table. "Put it all down," he demanded. "Positions, dispersements, guns, strength of air coverage— everything."

Hardshaw laid the pencil aside. "Just one more thing, Captain." The native's face became suffused into bronze casting. Hardshaw continued quickly. "The others. They despise me for what I'm doing. Kill them—now!"

The captain relaxed, in an evil smile. "We shall kill them—eventually."

Hardshaw stood up. "I must see it done. I cannot go back to my lines with the slightest danger that one of them will return. You must shoot them now!"

The little captain became friendly, and with smirking lips, gave a jerky bow. "Yank," he said, "what a pity you are not a Partisan! You would have much to offer the Party."

Hardshaw looked on while Joe, Mike, Solly and Spud were cut loose and dragged to the edge of camp. He watched the soldiers push them to their knees, then shoot them in the back of their heads. He closed his eyes in momentary anguish. He saw again the old gang back home for whom he had named his crew. He saw his home town, the corner drug store, he heard his mother calling from the kitchen, he felt the soft wind from the Texas plain on his cheek. And he saw in a brief flash all the gay lights of all the great capitals of the world . . . but here he would leave the ashes of his last campfire.

He opened his eyes and looked down at the little Communist captain. "I have no information for you," he said quietly. "My comrades are beyond your torture now. Do what you like with me."

A MEMENTO OF EDGAR ALLAN POE

EDITORIAL NOTE:

This story was written by two people. Mr. Burke's share in it is self-evident. The rest was narrated to him (he claims) by Edgar Allan Poe. A careful check of Mr. Poe's writings will show that every line is taken from the master narrator's stories, poems and letters. The result is an ingenious mosaic of authentic Poe and a new Edgar Allan Poe tale, reflecting a problem and a terror that were central to the life of this tortured genius.

"I beg your pardon, sir," the tall stranger said in pure Virginia English, "this is the Rue Morgue?"

I looked up at the street sign and somewhat to my surprise saw that it was. I knew that the street was in the neighborhood of my hotel but I did not know exactly how I had come to be here. That afternoon my wife and I had arrived in Paris (for a few days of much needed vacation, in order to recover from the "Berlin claustrophobia" which periodically overtook those confined in the Soviet surrounded former Reich capital). She had pleaded a strange dizziness (some months later our son, Dickie, was born) and insisted that I take the evening out alone. After leaving the Folies Bergères I had gone on a little celebration. It was now three in the morning and I was weaving my uncertain way back to my hotel and my wife. The street on which I had encountered the tall stranger was dark and as still as a tomb. I was glad to meet someone speaking good, if somewhat stilted, English.

"That's what the sign says," I replied, trying to steady it in y Pernod-ridden vision. "Don't you know where you are?"

"It's been a long time, and there have been a lot of altera-tions."

"Well, this is Rue Morgue, all right," I assured him, and started walking in what I presumed to be the direction of my hotel.

The stranger fell in beside me, and it was then that I recog-nized him. We came to a small bar. "I don't know about you, Mr. Poe," I said. "I'm going to have myself a nightcap. Will you join me?"

We sat across a worn stone-top table, facing each other. I could easily understand why so many women had fallen madly in love with the poet. His eyes were striking—large and bril-liant; his features good—a straight nose, firm mouth, broad forehead from which his fine brown hair flowed thick and wavy. He was wearing a white neckcloth and a dark cape which, I noticed when he threw it back over his shoulder, was lined with red satin. I ordered a Pernod but he would have only a glass of light port.

"But I understand, Mr. Poe, that you, er . . . imbibe heart-ily of the stronger stuff."

He smiled. "Old Rufus Griswold. He wrote the first biogra-phy of me, you know. Poor Rufus. He was a frustrated preacher, wanted to be a writer. He hated me. However, I for-gave him a long time ago. I'm afraid he stretched my occa-sional drinking all out of proportion."

"Something ought to be done about it!" I said indignantly, and drank my Pernod.

"Griswold wasn't entirely wrong, though he did overstress my unfortunate habit. The truth of the matter is that my delicate constitution couldn't stand the shock of alcohol; a small portion of it produced disastrous effects on me.

"I recall one grievous occasion upon which I permitted my-self to fall under the evil influence to a dangerous degree," he continued in his clear, melodious voice. "On this occasion I

was suffering the horrible first stages of creeping despair. Th.
was the hideous dropping of the veil, the bitter lapse int
sobriety. This was the drab return from that gilded, riotous,
gay, incontinent world of the inebriated. Utter depression
bore down upon my soul and a sinking, a sickness of heart,
possessed me. My nerves, sheltered thinly underneath my
burning skin, were sharp as a razor's edge and throbbed
fiercely, and my mind sought to wander beyond the bounds
of my skull, as if anxious to flee this quaking, shaking, pre-
carious coil. My flesh shuddered and my soul burned at the
very thought, the *hope,* that I could endure this terrible,
mortifying period of recovery. But endure it I could and
would! I had promised Helen.

"While raven-winged hours dragged endlessly through the
forepart of a dull, ashen and soundless December night, I
tossed restlessly, desperately craving sleep, in the cramped upstairs room of the little cottage. Beside my bed a single flame
upreared itself from a tarnished candelabrum and cast shadows that withered and loomed on the walls. With horrible
clarity I realized that sleep, that soft embalmer of the soul,
was to be denied me; and the stark realization of what this
irrepressible wakefulness would bring bolted me upright on
the pillows, trembling with apprehension. Oh, could I but
hold the mantle of sweet, deft unconsciousness up before me
until this loathsome state passed! I stared at the jaded tapestry
which appeared now close, now far away, and in a gloomy
state of self-pity and great depression bemoaned my plight.

"It had started at the Earl House Bar, in Providence. On
the night before, I had delivered my most successful lecture
on *The Poetic Principle* before the Franklin Lyceum. There
were eighteen hundred enthusiastic auditors, and I hoped I
had distinguished myself; for on the following Monday she—
the Helen of a thousand of my most exquisite dreams—had
promised to become my wife. Late that afternoon I was to
meet her at the library. I had hours to pass, and so had wan-

dered gaily and with bright spirits into the bar of the Earl House, where I was lodging. A group of young men with whom I had struck up a casual acquaintance during my visit in Providence were imbibing a light wine. With cheerful voices and warm overtures they insisted that I join them in a drink. In my state of felicity (a rare mood indeed), a new strength, a great confidence of will, encompassed me, over which by no goading of the imagination could I envision myself again fallen into a state of drunkenness. Surely I was man enough, morally, spiritually, physically, to take a drink, just *one* drink, and then let it alone. So—I blush with shame at this confession—I again succumbed.

"The ramifications of the debauch which followed are vague and desultory in my memory. How much I drank and where the whimsy of liquor led me and to what degree of degradation I sank, the Giver of all good mercifully spared me the knowledge forevermore.

"But all things must end: the most exquisite and the most outlandish. At length I regained sufficient sobriety to see Helen, and presented myself, in an extremely harassed condition, at her house. She was at once resolved that her influence in reforming me would be futile and that her marriage with me could bring no benefits to either, and nothing but misery for both; and she added, yet not without solace, that my infringement of my promise had released her from her own. I beseeched, I entreated, I supplicated, I pleaded with her, yet she remained obdurate and countermanded the publication of the marriage banns.

"I could not and would not believe this was to be the quietus to our love, for had we not already planned to be together for the remainder of our lives? I thought of our first interview, in the cemetery, where under the stars her pale, eager face became lighted with a fine spiritual expression, and the dreaminess shone in her deep-set eyes that looked over and beyond you but never at you. I told her that naught ever had stirred me as when her eyes first rested on mine for one brief moment, and I felt, for the first time in my life, and tremblingly acknowledged, the existence of spiritual influences altogether out of reach of the reason. I confessed that afterwards, on visits to her in this very parlor in which I now knelt beside her, my brain reeled beneath the intoxicating spell of her presence; and as she passed to and fro about the room—now sitting by my side, now far away, now standing with her hand resting on the back of my chair, while the preternatural thrill of her touch vibrated through the senseless wood into my heart—while she moved restlessly about the room, as if a deep sorrow or a most profound joy haunted her bosom, it became clear to me that without her the remainder of my life would be but a voyage in sadness and misery.

"After desperate moments that left me swaying on the brink of despair, our hands clasped, and my whole soul shook with a tremulous ecstasy.

" 'I love you—' she whispered in low accents.

"Presently then, she again promised to marry me, but not at once; first, I must prove to her *beyond a doubt* that I could and would abstain from drink.

"I left Providence with my heart uplifted once more, and while the boat was arriving in New York, in order to re-affirm to Helen that her trust was not misspent, I dispatched a letter to her. I wrote in part:

" '. . . It is five o'clock and the boat is just being made fast at the wharf. I shall start on the first train that leaves New York at 7 for Fordham. I write this to show you that I have not *dared* to break my promise to you. And now, Dearest Helen, be true to me . . .'

"I did not tell her how, at this very moment, my quaking frame craved just one small potion— (a whisker of the cat that had scratched me)—and how enticingly, how with such singular *camaraderie*, the swinging doors of the establishment across yon cobblestone pavement enjoined me thither. But stout was I in my resolutions and in my love for Helen—and stick by my guns I would—so, I took the seven o'clock train for home.

"Throughout the day I suffered as cannot be recorded by voice or pen. My spirits sank to even greater depths and my fortitude wavered. I paced the floors and dreamed of and planned for the time when Helen would come to the little cottage in Fordham as my beloved wife. I conjured up and expounded a thousand reasons why I should not and *would* not touch drink again—ever. How much of my reasoning against the evil was *rationalization,* I will not attempt to expound to you. In my state of reform and repentance, however, I explained to myself, in an attempt at justification, just why I had allowed the Demon to possess me in the first place.

"It had begun, to a serious degree, six years before in Philadelphia. One evening, when my precious and frail wife Virginia—whom I loved as no man ever loved before—while playing the harp and singing had ruptured a blood vessel. Her life was despaired of. I took leave of her forever and underwent all the agonies of her death. She recovered partially and I again hoped. At the end of a year the vessel broke again. I went through precisely the same scene. Again in about a year afterward. Then again—again—and even once more again, at varying intervals. Each time I felt the agonies of her death, and at each accession of the disorder I loved her more dearly and clung to her life with more desperate pertinacity. But I am constitutionally sensitive and nervous to a very unusual degree. I became insane, with long intervals of horrible sanity. During these fits of obscurity I drank, God only knows how often or how much. (As a matter of course, my enemies referred the insanity to the drink rather than the drink to the insanity.) Then when I had, indeed, nearly abandoned all hope of a permanent cure, I found one in the *death* of my wife. This I can and did endure as becomes a man; it was the terrible never-ending oscillation between hope and despair which I could *not* longer have endured, without total loss of reason. In the death of what was my life, then, I received a new, but—oh, God! how melancholy an existence! Work offered a measure of solace and forgetfulness. It was in this fruitful period that I produced *Annabel Lee,* which I believe to be, in all literature, the supreme expression of love—our love. We had loved each other so much that *God's highest order of angels* envied her and me.

"The austere day at length buried itself in gloom. I lighted a candle, ensconced it in a huge leaden candelabrum, and swooping up my great, tortoise-colored cat Catarina, went and threw myself on the bed. Catarina consolingly reclined in my arms. I lay, wooing and beseeching sleep, yet the oiled lid would not close over the casket of my soul. The hours waned and waned away.

"How long I lay in a state of quaking apprehension, dreading and wondering, I cannot determine. Suddenly I sprang upright from my pillow. The blood in my body congealed in my veins and my hair erected itself on the roots in my head. The walls had hurled a tremulous, husky and loud voice at me.

" 'Reynolds!' it shouted. 'Reynolds! Oh, Reynolds!'

"For long minutes I harkened, peering into the shadows that writhed on the walls and in the sombre tapestry, my recreant heart audibly beating. At length, sanity asserted itself and I realized it was my own voice that I had heard. Out of what *must* have been a dream I had shouted for J. N. Reynolds, the explorer who had given me the idea and much of the detail that went into *The Narrative of Arthur Gordon Pym, of Nantucket.*

"After a time I became distinctly aware of a gentle footfall upon the carpet, and near my bed; and in a second thereafter, I saw clearly the body of John Allan, whose foster child I had been and who for the past fourteen years had lain beside my kindly foster mother in a Richmond cemetery. From the swingng of his arms, his protruding paunch, his fat and stubby hands, I recognized him. The face I had not yet perceived, but in a second more my burning glances fell upon what should have been it. But there was none, or more properly, there was none which I could see; for the entire head was enveloped in frequent rolls of linen bandages in the precise manner of that of a mummy.

"Shaking off this apparition, I struggled to my feet. Cold globules of perspiration were gathering on my forehead. I took the candelabrum in hand, preparatory to going downstairs to await the dawn, sitting up. This notion, however, was never carried out; for framed in the doorway and prohibiting my passage was a giant ape. A singular feature about his face caught and held my fancy: he was possessed of but a solitary eye, the other having been gouged out, leaving a gory, sepulchral empty socket. The monster advanced toward me when, overcome with maddening fear, I sank to the floor. A second later I felt the brute's gigantic foot on my chest, crushing me. Then an ebon black funnel descended and closed over me.

"To the deck of a phantom ship I am securely bound by a strap that passes in many convolutions about my limbs and body, leaving at liberty only my head. By dint of much exertion I can take in my surroundings. I am, as far as can be ascertained by much twisting and turning, the only occupant aboard the vessel, which is under full sail and pressing at great speed westward, ever toward the setting sun. As the ship rolls and dips with great swells I can determine that it is headed toward the edge of the world, where the sea cascades into space! The earth, then, *is* flat after all! Over the high, black mountainous ridge I am certain to go, and I realize with horror that I am utterly helpless to do anything about it. Straining at my bounds only brings thrusting pains in my chest. An extraordinarily large wave bears me upward and careens the ship in such a manner that I glimpse into the downward slope of the cascade. What I see brings new horror. The wild waste of liquid whirls and sweeps in terrific grandeur down into a mighty and tremendous maelstrom. As it is, I involuntarily close my eyes in awe. The lids clench themselves together as if in a spasm. 'Reynolds!' I try to scream but the sound dies unarticulated in my throat.

"Upon opening my eyes, I behold a huge and magnificent rainbow, like a narrow and tottering bridge which Mussulmen say is the only pathway between Time and Eternity. With a full bosom of woe, I seek to resolve myself to the fate which lies suddenly ahead. But I am not to be spared further torment *first*. And now, amid all my infinite miseries, I become aware of another presence. Turning my head, I perceive it is the giant gorilla. He is dragging a black, oblong box, about six feet in length by two and a half in breadth, along the deck. Depositing the box near the railing, he tears off the lid with his great stout claws. Out of it comes John Allan. While I gaze on the scene in the extremity of astonishment, the mummy-headed man passes several turns of a three-inch rope first around the box, then around his middle. In another instant both body and box are in the sea, disappearing at once.

"The giant ape, in whose solitary eye lurks a singular hatred belonging more to a human fiend than to a beast, strides toward me, his long hairy arms skipping the deck. Grasping me by the arm, he gives it a violent twist, tearing it off at the elbow. The pain is sharp and agonizing, but only at intervals of several seconds apart. Out of the gory stub, which the fiend gazes upon stupidly with his solitary orb, fall large ovoids of brilliant and ruby-colored blood, which after striking the deck become transformed into miniature transparent coffins; and encased in each of these is a beautiful maiden, white-shrouded and lifeless.

"While I study in a state of numbed amazement the indescribable loveliness of these inert creatures, the ape produces out of nowhere a full-sized coffin in the likeness of the others, except that this one is lidless. This he holds over me for a moment; then by gradual degrees he lowers it so that, though lying on my back, I am face down *inside* the casket. Almost immediately I begin smothering. There sits upon my very heart an incubus of utter anguish. I realize that within the stifling confines of my coffin I am turning pale as the tenants of the miniature tombs. Gasping and choking, I can plainly feel Death crowding the spirit out of my breast. Death! And with wild alarm I suddenly realize I am to die. But not in this horrible manner! No! Let me die in the light, where there is air, surrounded by friends and loved ones. And as if in answer to my wild and fervent yearning, the blackness lifts and there is light.

"I found that when I had collapsed a table had become up-set, throwing the heavy leaden candelabrum onto my chest, while the burning candle lay in the crook of my arm and dropped its hot tallow on my uncovered elbow. My weak heart had been acting up and had caused a certain spasm in my breast. Moreover Catarina had wandered back into the room (having been frightened away no doubt at my hysterical call-ing for Reynolds) and was now sitting calmly upon me with her face imminently close to my lips, stealing away the very air from my mouth!

"I douched my face in cold water and resumed pacing the house; but finally the realization that I was unable longer to suffer in this diabolical limbo made itself manifest, and I began considering avenues of escape. Pushing open the shutters of the tiny window I peered out into the oppressive gloom, search-ing long and profoundly into the deep, black night. Out there, somewhere, was escape from the *horrors* which claimed me. Overpowered by an intense and dreadful apprehension of what might *yet* beset me, I resolved to arouse myself from this pitiable condition. I fumbled in the drawer of my dresser, and—thank God!—it was still there. I took a long pull at the bottle; there was a terrible moment of uncertainty, but after some gagging and retchings it stayed down. In a moment I

took another quaff—then another—another—and still anothe
A warmth began at the pit of my stomach and spread, floating
my spirits to brighter realms. The dregs of the bottle sent
them fairly soaring. I looked at my hands; they were steady
now. I ground my teeth until I heard them grate. I was standing in the middle of the room, master of myself completely.
What next?

"What of Helen: With a twinge of mortification and a shrug
I resigned myself to her loss. I cursed the bottle because it was
empty and flung it against the wall where it shattered into a
thousand fragments. I wound my neckcloth in place, drew on
my greatcoat, swept out of the room, scrambled down the
stairs and plunged out into the night, swiftly onward, I well
knew, toward the edge of the world. And to see my Helen—
nevermore."

When my distinguished companion had finished, we both
sat in silence for a few minutes. "A sad story, Mr. Poe," I said
finally. "Being a newspaperman, I suppose I ought to ask 'May
I quote you, sir?' "

"Certainly, if you like."

"How about some sort of confirmation?"

He smiled, and slipped a sleeve band off his arm and pressed
it into my hand. It was one of those garter-looking affairs
similar to those used by old-time editors and printers to hold
their sleeves up on their arms so they would not get soiled by
the ink pots and inked surfaces of the type and plates. Then he
glanced at the window; it was getting light outside. "Now I
must leave you. I have an appointment and cannot be late."
So saying he was gone.

I went to my hotel, missing my way several times. At last
I found my room, the door, the keyhole. I laid Mr. Poe's
memento on the night stand and went to sleep.

Next morning I awoke fully dressed. My wife was standing
over my bed with the sleeve band in her hand. I was about to
tell her the amazingly remarkable story I would write that day.

Then my eyes fell upon the thing. I had not realized the night before to what a remarkable degree Mr. Poe's sleeve band resembled the pink garters worn by the Folies Bergères girls. No word came out of my open mouth.

When my wife reads this in print, she will know for the first time the true story of Mr. Poe's memento.

THE PAINTED DOODLE BUG

CAROLE GLANCED at the terminal clock. In fifteen minutes Robert's plane would be in. As the long red sweep-second hand pinched off the seconds she became nervous. She felt her legs weaken and sat down to calm herself. From behind the circular glass-enclosed lobby she saw the enormous sweep of Tempelhof Airdrome, the long runways criss-crossing the green-brown field, and the hulks of bombed-out buildings in the far background. It was here that she had said good-bye to Robert twenty long months ago. In a few minutes she would see him, tall and with his slow smile, coming up the stone steps looking eagerly for her.

He would take her in his arms even more eagerly. But what would he do when she told him? Would he still want her? Would he take her to America? *Could* he take her now? The time had come when her husband, who had just returned from Korea, must know all about her Communist affiliations.

Oh, why, why hadn't she told him before! But she knew the answer. The new-found courage Robert had brought her since he had come into her life had vanished that day she watched him disappear into the cabin of the America-bound plane. Remembering now, it seemed such a long, long time ago. Though the day she first met Robert seemed like only yesterday.

She had opened the door to the knock at her room over the bombed-out garage where she lived and there he was, standing solid on his two feet, which were a little wide apart. That was Robert, always solid and sure and firm.

"I'm Sergeant Evans from the Quartermaster," he had said.

"Where are the owners of the house next door? We're going to derequisition it."

Dead, she had told him. Both her parents had died in the last big bomb raid on Berlin. "In that case," he had told her, "I guess we'll have to derequisition it to you."

"But what will I do with it?" she had asked him.

He stood there like a tower, she thought, a tall tower of strength, looking down gently and comfortingly into her soft, tea-colored eyes. Then he looked at the faint line between her eyebrows that should not be there, on that face so young. His eyes swept her soft, light brown hair. Then noted the moist sheen of her lips that made them seem soft and warm and cool and tender all at the same time. And he saw the sad curve of them, too.

"You could rent the house," he said, "I know a man. An airline official. He's looking for a house. Yours ought to suit him fine. Like me to help you?"

That's the way it had started. From that very first moment Carole borrowed from Robert the courage she needed to live again. Soon the sad curve of her lips disappeared, and on her face was a look of gladness, as if she had made some marvelous discovery. She was in love with him.

It was near the end of the Berlin blockade, when everyone knew the Russians were licked and would give up soon, that Robert told her he wanted to marry her. They were walking home from the Harnack House in the darkness of a mild May evening. He put his arm gently but firmly around her shoulder.

"Carole," he said, "many of us will be going home soon. How would you like to go with me—as my wife?" He said this as he did all things, kindly, surely and confidently.

They did not get married until late summer. There were many papers to fill out and long weeks to wait until things were properly in file. Robert borrowed a jalopy from his friend, Corporal Tommy Manson, and they drove down the *Autobahn* to Frankfurt, over to Karlsruhe and into the Black

Forest. They found a little rustic inn, sitting like a precious old jewel in the dark green setting of the forest, and stayed there for a week. Then Robert took her to Stuttgart and Munich, where they had a go at the American and German night spots. Afterwards they got in the jalopy and took off for Garmisch and Berchtesgaden.

At the hotel in Berchtesgaden Robert got up the nerve to put on the bold pajamas he bought at the PX in Stuttgart. Carole burst into laughter.

"Are those bugs!" she shrieked, pointing to the large, garishly colored predatory beetles adorning Robert's pajamas.

"Not *bugs*. They're scarabs. They bring luck. That's what the girl in the PX told me."

"They're bugs," she laughed. "Doodle bugs!"

With arms akimbo he happily looked at her. He was smiling too. "Carole, my darling," he said, "don't ever stop laughing. Never have I seen you so beautiful. You've laughed so little in your time."

He took her in his arms, tousled her hair, and laughing together they sank onto the bed. He pressed her hard against the great doodle bugs—or scarabs. The question at this point remained undecided.

Next day their honeymoon was cut short by a cablegram saying Robert's mother was gravely ill. They hurried back to Berlin and Robert's C. O. arranged for him to return home via a Military Air Transport Service plane that left immediately. A few days later Robert telephoned the sad news of his mother's death.

Then a letter said he had been given an extension to straighten out the family affairs. He telephoned again to tell Carole the good news that he had been assigned to a big army post on the West Coast. She would be coming to join him there soon. Just a few more papers to fill out. She realized now that she should have told him all at the very beginning.

Her two younger brothers, Gerhard and Albert, had gone
to the Russian Sector to live and had become violent active
Communist Youth leaders. Thoroughly indoctrinated, they
were arrogant, bold, defiant, and in a way courageous. They
did things others dared not, and were constantly in the newspapers because of their many bold deeds. During a West Sector
rally Gerhard climbed the old burned-out Reichstag building,
which is at one of the squares where the rally was held, and
brazenly emplanted two huge red flags. Then he cleverly
escaped back into the East Sector through a cordon of several
hundred West Sector policemen and Allied MP's. Albert,
equally bold, sailed an old Luftwaffe glider right over HICOG,
Headquarters of the American High Commissioner, and
dropped bales of Communist propaganda leaflets. The Communist newspapers in Berlin screamed Gerhard's and Albert's
names.

Whenever Carole sat down to write Robert she fully intended telling him all about her brothers. But she never quite
got the courage to do so. Since Robert had gone away her
courage had dwindled; she seldom laughed any more, and the
old fears, plus the new ones created almost daily by Gerhard
and Albert, encircled her again. Anyway, she rationalized, they
would be together soon and it would be much easier to tell
him then.

The war in Korea came and Robert's outfit was one of the
first to go. Each day with the war news she died, each night
she roamed the dark Gehenna of fear and doubt of what
horrible news the morrow would bring.

One day the *Tägliche Rundschau,* the main Berlin Communist paper, ran a picture of her with the caption "Comrade
Carole, sister of the famous Gerhard and Albert Stalmol."

That same day she received through the mail a Communist
Party card, properly enrolling her into the Party. HICOG
acted quickly, since she lived in the American Sector. They

picked her up, and for days she was interrogated unmercifully. Finally they let her go, but she knew that she was under surveillance day and night.

So, as Carole watched the minutes click away in the terminal she trembled. At least, she told herself, trying to hold back the flood of desperation, she would not tell Robert until they were in the taxi. It would be a long ride to her home and she must have those precious minutes together with him as they used to be. Mercifully, Robert had not learned anything about it, she told herself, for HICOG had kept it quiet and besides, for the public record, her name had been Stalmol.

When the plane taxied up and was positioned, Carole saw Robert, taller than the other passengers, coming down the unloading ramp. She ran down the concrete steps from the waiting room and sped to him. He dropped the baggage and packages he was loaded down with and swept her up in his arms. He swung her around, holding her tightly. Carole's pain and loneliness born of waiting ages for this precious moment melted away in his first words. "Carole! My own darling!"

During the taxi ride to her apartment she tried to tell him about the whole mess but got nowhere. Every time she tried to speak he kissed her and opened another gift he'd brought. When they reached her building she still hadn't told him. She led him up the stairs with panic in her stomach and death in her heart. Words stuck in her throat.

She unlocked the door, helped Robert in with the bags and packages. Then all of a sudden Carole heard herself talking. Words came fast and furious. She knew she was talking in circles and now and then was conscious of the words Gerhard and Albert. In the end the whole story was out. And the couch where Robert had been was empty. He was gone!

She couldn't even sob. She merely dropped to the couch completely numbed. Not with shock, for this was what she had expected all along. But with all the old fear and loneliness redoubled a thousand times.

It was only minutes before Robert came back, but for Carole it was centuries. The door opened and there he was, and smiling.

"Oh, Robert!" Carole burst out, rising into his arms.

"I know, I know," he said softly. "Soon, my darling, you will be away from this dark, brooding city. Away from all that has haunted you all your life. Then you will feel free and firm and strong. No more uncertainty and doubt and fright. No more fear—ever. Carole, I knew the whole story in Washington.

"In time you will come to understand this. You were really innocent of any wrong-doing, and you had nothing to fear all along. That's the simple American way. HICOG has exonerated you and you're cleared in Washington, too. We can leave immediately for home."

"Home." Carole repeated the word as if it held the promise of heaven itself. "Home." She said it again and it charmed her whole face.

"You know," he scolded her mockingly, "in your frustration you made me leave the most important package in the taxi. He was pulling away when I got down the stairs." Robert opened the package.

It was a large toy beetle, painted in red, green, yellow and blue. Carole suddenly became as bright as the colors themselves. "See," he said. "It's a doodle bug."

"No, Robert, it's not a doodle bug," Carole said, smiling brilliantly. "It's a scarab. It brings luck."

MURDER HAD TENDER FINGERS

IT WAS half past five when Renate finished packing. She stacked the bags beside the door. Joe's B-4 bag, stuffed until it was almost round, sat atop his foot locker, which Joe had personally packed with the souvenirs he had gathered during his five-year sojourn in Germany as a War Department civilian employee. Renate glanced at the little clock that ticked busily on the coffee table before the fireplace; then she went to the window. Outside it was already dark, and the November fog lay in great whorls across the park and, boiling up, partially shrouded the I. G. Farben Building two blocks away. What was keeping Karl? He knew he had to be there before Joe came home.

Renate's steely blue eyes softened a little when she thought of Karl. It had been a long devious trail for them, but now a bright future lay ahead, America and plenty of money to spend. There was just the matter of getting rid of her husband, Joe, first. Karl could be relied upon. She remembered their Hitler Jugend days together; and after that how trim and handsome blond Karl was in his SS uniform. She recalled, too, her service as assistant to an experimental surgeon in Buchenwald Concentration Camp. Totally without experience, she had gotten the assignment through a sly romance with a bigwig Nazi in Berlin. The ghost of a smile crossed her lips as she thought of how she had completely fooled even Karl. Germany held no future for two such people. The decency of the German people itself rejected them. Renate saw this perhaps more clearly than did Karl.

The doorbell rang, a short furtive ring. Karl! Renate opened the door and slid briefly into his arms.

"Are you sure no one saw you?"

"I came through the alley," Karl said. "No one saw me. *Bestimmt!*"

"Karl!" There was a commanding ring in her voice. "No more German! Only English from now on."

"Sorry, my darling," he said, substituting "my darling" for the usual *mein Liebling*. He smiled a hard smile. But it didn't seem hard on his unfeeling, arrogant face. "Is everything set?"

"Everything is arranged. Joe's orders have been issued for us to leave for Bremerhaven in the morning, where we take the *General Rose* for New York."

She led him to an alcove at the far end of the room, drew the curtains. "Joe will be here any minute now. I'll let you know when. Then be quick and sure."

In a few minutes Renate heard Joe's key in the lock. She met him in the middle of the room, the overhead light, as she knew it would, playing its beams in her smooth, yellow hair and producing shadows in her high cheeks. He held her at arm's length, smiled at her loveliness. Then he gathered her in his arms and kissed her.

"What a day," he sighed, sinking into a large easy chair. "But we're practically on our way, honey. I've seen everybody and done everything I was supposed to do. Including this." He threw a large pack of green bills on the coffee table. "The American Express gave it all to me in U. S. currency. Renate, honey, until we were married three weeks ago—I confess it now—I never believed you'd really go through with it. I guess I'm pretty lucky."

She smiled and brushed his cheek teasingly with her red lips.

"First thing we'll do when we get to America is buy a

home," Joe went on thoughtfully. "I've worked hard and saved my money these five years. For the rest of your life, honey, I want you to have a fine roof over your head. Not like that bombed-out hovel you've been living in next door." Renate's eyes were fastened on the money. She hadn't heard much of what he said. "How much is there, Joe?"

"You mercenary wench!" he laughed, and mockingly clipped her chin with his fist.

Catching herself, she said, "I'm sorry, Joe, my darling." Then she pressed his head to her bosom, released him the moment she felt his ardor rise. She gave him her most provocative smile.

"Relax a little, darling," she ordered in a soft voice, while she passed her long, white, tender fingers caressingly over his cheek, down around his chin and up the nape of his neck.

Joe closed his eyes and sank deeper into the big chair, as always, when she did this. She signalled with her eyes and Karl started forward. The doorbell rang.

"Who on earth could that be!" Her voice was a razor's edge.

"Why so jumpy?" Joe asked, opening his eyes. "Go and see, honey."

It was Lieutenant Herman Thorpe, Joe's friend in the Engineer Corps. "Just got back from Munich today," he announced. "Sorry I missed the wedding. It's a bit late, but congratulations!" He slapped Joe on the shoulder, shook hands. He boldly kissed Renate on both cheeks. Then he flopped in a chair. "Break out with a drink, *Deutsche Frau!* You don't get rid of me without a parting libation."

While Renate was in the kitchen getting glasses and the nearly empty bottle of bourbon, she heard the two friends talking. Suddenly they burst out in a chorus of loud laughter. When she returned Lieutenant Thorpe was saying, "That's the army. You put in a request for a simple little thing. Noth-

ing happens. You forget all about it. Six months later, when
is doesn't matter any more, it comes through!" They both
laughed again.

Lieutenant Thorpe finished his drink and, sensing Renate's
impatience, wished them luck, promised to write, said good-
bye, and left.

"You must rest a little while, Joe," Renate insisted. "You're
worn out from all that running around today."

She brought his pipe, and while he smoked she stood behind
his chair, stroking his cheeks. Joe never knew when Renate
took away her tender fingers and the hardened hands of Karl
clamped around his neck.

Renate got out her make-up kit, which she used when she
got a bit part in a play, and proceeded to darken Karl's eyebrows and hair to a likeness of that of the dead American
who still sat, with pipe in a limp hand, in the big easy chair
with its back to the alcove.

"Good!" she finally said, looking from the still face of Joe
to Karl. "With his papers, we cannot possibly fail!"

The doorbell rang. Renate drew in a sharp breath. Karl
stood stiffly, his cold face hardening under the disguise deftly
applied by Renate, his powerful hands clenched.

"Quickly!" she commanded in a sharp whisper. "Get behind
the curtain!"

Renate went to the bedroom, kicked off her shoes, pulled on
a robe over her suit, rumpled her hair, switched off the lights
and went to the door. It was Lieutenant Thorpe.

"Sorry," he apologized when he saw Renate through the
crack in the door. "I had a crazy notion you and Joe would
like to take a last fling at the joints in dear old Frankfurt
tonight."

"Joe's sound asleep. He was dead tired," she said with a
little yawn.

"Sure, sure," the embarrassed Lieutenant mumbled. "Stupid of me to bother you." He turned to go, but came back.

"By the way, here's the copy of that work order for Joe. I forgot to leave it." She slipped the folded paper in her jacket pocket.

Renate stood at the door until she heard Lieutenant Thorpe get in his car, start the motor and drive away.

Afterward she and Karl carried Joe's body down the stairs and along the apartment building to the pile of rubble that was once the living room of the war-damaged apartment, where Renate had lived until she married Joe. In the thickening fog they buried Joe underneath the broken brick and concrete.

Karl gave a scornful laugh. "Joke on the Amis. One buried in their own mess!"

Ten days later the *General Rose* docked in Brooklyn and "Joseph Arnoldson" and his German bride walked confidently down the gangplank. Cleared through customs, they took a taxi to New York and checked in at a fashionable midtown hotel.

During the weeks that followed, Renate had an exciting spree of buying, while Karl spent pleasant afternoons charming the exquisite ladies who frequent the stylish bars.

One day while their cab moved and stopped and moved again in the traffic stream, far behind a siren began wailing. Neither paid any attention, until the black police limousine, its siren now bleating in short snarling command, swept around and blocked their cab.

At the police station, when they were searched, a folded sheet of paper was found in Renate's jacket pocket, the jacket she had worn the night they murdered Joe. The paper was a copy of an Army Engineer Corps Work Order authorizing the immediate, full and complete repairing of the bomb damage to her old apartment.

She remembered, now, that months ago Joe had asked his friend, Lieutenant Thorpe, to "stretch a point and have Renate's apartment rebuilt."

THE TIGER AND THE WOLF

GONZALEZ, Dictator of the little Latin republic of Arana, unfavorably known to his long suffering people as *El Tigre,* paced up and down beside the great plane, hidden in the jungle, which bore the inscription "Good Neighbor" in English and Spanish script.

He cursed and fumed. Would General Zatapol never come!

Zatapol, foreigner, soldier of fortune, opportunist, was *El Tigre's* chief of secret police and head of Arana's tiny air force, and with good reason had won the appellation of *El Lobo.* Hunting in close accord, the Tiger and the Wolf had ruled and robbed and murdered in Arana for ten years. Now the people had revolted and the army was with them. It was time for the Tiger and the Wolf to take to distant timber.

Gonzalez swore aloud and ground a shiny boot in the dirt. He looked at the descending sun. They must take off before darkness. Even with the skill of his two personal pilots it would be risky. Although Zatapol was a first-rate pilot, he had recently taken to boozing heavily and for this reason Gonzalez did not trust him with the task of getting the huge plane out of the narrow clearing and safely out of Arana. But where was the vain scoundrel? Probably putting on his best uniform and all his medals. Gonzalez groaned.

He turned a startled face toward the city as the evening breeze brought to his ears the song of machine-gun fire and a chorus of wild yells. *The mob is storming the palace,* he thought and smiled grimly. That would mean the end of Enrique, who, as his double, had been left to face revolting army and mob. He had given Enrique his instructions. He was to remain in

96

the palace, just inside the balcony fronting the square, until the loyal palace guards were drivin in. Then, as *El Tigre,* he was to step out on the balcony and try to placate the mob with a speech, promising anything and everything in the way of reforms—even to the resignation of *El Tigre* as Dictator. If, however, he failed, he was to hurry to the secret flying field and accompany his chief in exile. Enrique, with tears in his eyes and hand on his heart, had promised to do so; for, as Gonzalez knew, Enrique had long cherished the secret belief that he could function as Dictator far better than the man who employed him as his double to be shot at. This was his chance to prove it.

Gonzalez had not the slightest doubt but that Enrique had been cut to pieces by machine-gun fire the instant he appeared on the balcony, and he fervently hoped so. The sentimental fool! Ambitious idiot!—who dared become jealous of *El Tigre.*

The uproar cityward died down to spasmodic rifle shots and the snarling of a mob intent upon looting. *The idiots think they have killed El Tigre and now they are plundering the palace,* he mused with a sardonic smile. *Gives us more time to get away.*

He looked fondly at the giant plane. A pilot showed an anxious face at the window of the cockpit. The great four-engined ship with half a dozen smaller ones had been a gift from the Good Neighbor. Also there had been a loan of $3,000,000. He chuckled. The other planes stood dismantled and most of the money was going with him in chests already stowed in the plane.

"Ha! General Zatapol!"

The general, immaculately uniformed, strode hurriedly across the clearing from the jungle, the sun's fading rays glinting on his bemedaled chest. The little Dictator, plump and swarthy, showered his tall partner with abuse as they mounted to the belly of the plane.

Soon it was evident that *El Tigre* had not underestimated

his personal pilots, for they maneuvered the plane out of the woods and were already over the sea, leaving Arana behind. The Dictator relaxed.

Pleased with the happy progress thus far, he became effusive. "General, take a good look at Arana," he said. "You will never see it again. You cannot be sad for it is not your country. I am not sad either. Although it is my country, I have no further use for it. Now I shall tell you a little of my plan, but not all. I have prepared a place for us in a distant friendly People's Republic where we shall live in comfort and luxury for the rest of our lives. Long ago I prepared for just such an extremity. Alvarado and Guzman, whom I sent there, arranged everything down to the minutest detail. Nothing remains to be done."

For the first time since the plane took off, the tall one spoke: "Alvarado and Guzman? They were shot when they returned from that mission! You ordered them killed!"

"Why not?" snapped *El Tigre*. "Their job was completed— so their usefulness was gone. Besides, the success of my plan depended on absolute secrecy. I left nothing to chance. But let me continue. There will be, as I said, luxury and ease for us. Good food and wine and for me—maybe I'll even go into politics with our new friends." He leaned forward with a twinkle in his eye and poked the uniformed man in the ribs. "—And for you, my General, there will be all this and what you like most—girls! Plenty of them. The gold which rides with us guarantees all these things. You see, I have forgotten nothing."

The uniformed man opened his mouth to speak several times but his partner cut him off with his effusive enthusiasm. Finally, in desperation he blurted out, "Your Excellency, there's something I must tell you—"

"Ah, my General! I understand—you are worried." He jerked a thumb toward the cockpit. "Again I must remind you, I have forgotten nothing. They too have served their purpose.

They have brought us out of the danger zone. There is no need for them where we are going. General, go forward and send one of them here. Take his place in the cockpit. I'll give you the course to fly when I have finished with the pilots."

"But—Your Excellency! Listen to me! You must not." The bemedaled man was pale and trembling.

"Don't argue, General! Do as I tell you. *Madre de Dios!* Have I not done well so far? We cannot let sentiment interfere now. Go! Be quick about it!"

The tall man in the uniform hesitated, then went forward and in a few moments one of the pilots came aft and saluted. Without a word *El Tigre* opened the rear hatch, pointed to the black opening and motioned him to jump. The pilot peered down into twelve thousand feet of nothingness. He drew back and faced his hard master, refusing to die. The Dictator whipped out a revolver and brought its butt down violently on the pilot's head, shoved him through the open hatch into space.

Resolved to face no further opposition, he went forward, gun in hand. He stepped silently up behind the remaining pilot, held the muzzle of the gun at the base of his skull and pressed the trigger. The man slumped in his seat-harness, instantly dead.

"My God! My God! What have you done!" cried the fat uniform in the other seat.

The big plane slipped, skidded and banked crazily. Yet the trembling hands of the man would not take the controls.

"Your Excellency!" he wailed hysterically. "I've been trying to tell you. General Zatapol shot himself this morning. I am only his poor ignorant double—and God help us! I've never been inside an airplane before."

WHERE IS THE COAST OF FRANCE?

WHERE IS THE COAST OF FRANCE?

STANLEY WILSON turned on the water. It was cold. He swore. He went ahead with his shaving preparations anyway. Elizabeth would be coming in a few minutes now. The water ran over his hand and, as he held the razor to his face, down along his arm. He shivered, though it was a warm spring day. Then he laughed briefly as he thought of the many times he had shaved with ice-cold water—in training barracks, on board ships, in foxholes on far-away frozen hillsides.

He thought of the other times, too, before the Asian hillsides, when he had shaved with cold water, aboard the troopship that had carried him to England, in ill-equipped camps in the misty English dawn, the dawn that would then soon break over a gigantic machine moving across the channel. A machine of men, tank, cannon, and all sort of horrendous equipment designed to free the enslaved Continent.

Stanley Wilson shaved around the seared craters that was once a man's face, and remembered . . .

The boat was rocking and lurching. A salty breeze was rising, cold water sloshed over the gunwales. He shivered as they moved slowly and quietly in the pre-dawn out to the little islet where their plane awaited them. They had slept but little that night. After dark they had been given the final details of their mission. They were to cut the enemy's communications: snip telephone wires, blast message centers, destroy radio towers, wreck the enemy's nerve system. They were preceding the invasion by two hours. When their mission was completed, if any of them were still alive they were to try and join a unit which by this time—God willing—would have advanced beyond the beach. It was all very clear. And as the captain talked and pointed to the huge map on the wall it all seemed very simple. "You know this already," he said tonelessly, "but I mention it once again. You will be on your own. Accomplish your mission, then save yourselves if you can. This is no sporting event. If you meet the enemy, kill him before he kills you. Take no prisoners. Give no quarter. Any questions?"

Stanley Wilson knew what the others were thinking as the boat lurched and plowed through the water toward the waiting plane. *Survival. Get the mission over and get back to an Allied unit. Sure, some of the guys will be killed. Some of the others. But not me.*

He wondered if any of them were thinking what he was thinking. In college he had been considered an idealist. His professors approved; they liked him for it. But his friends considered him impractical, theoretical. "Stanley's got a head full of book sense," they often said, "but no common sense." He was here because he believed it was very necessary and cogently urgent, that the whole world be free. He believed he was fighting for just what the people in Washington and in London and in other great capitals had said they were fighting for. So he was thinking of what he had to do and how he had to do it, and why he was doing it. Also, he thought of Elizabeth, how heart-broken she would be if he should be killed.

The razor nicked his face and he winced. *Well, do I still believe in those people? Where are my ideals now? Don't I have a mission anymore? Oh, yes, I remember: to live and enjoy a decent life. Books, plays, friends and neighbors, television—and kids. Kids to live in a decent and free world. Or kids to die in vain for it?*

The plane winged low over the channel. It was a brief trip. How brief it was! And then down, quickly descending into the pre-dawn darkness. Was that the coast of France down there? The coastline, stretching like a huge bright-edged bolo blade, appeared beneath the plane, and then was gone. In a few minutes now Stanley Wilson, idealist, the student with a head full of book sense, would be fighting for that coastline and for the vast stretches of land and sky that lay beyond it. The captain was among them, issuing last minute instructions, checking equipment.

Equipment? he thought, looking at his face in the mirror. *Ah, equipment, that's the ticket. Equipment for a decent life. Such as Elizabeth, kids—and my ideals. Am I afraid? Why wasn't I afraid then? When we took our lives in our hands and threw them into space. Why am I afraid now?*

The captain looked at his watch, checked his map. He shouted the order. The door opened and man after man, with a great suffocating breath, stepped out into the dark sky. One by one they yelled the cry of the paratroops: GERONIMO!

It was exhilarating, exciting, dangerous. He was stout and brave, then—and he was whole. His chute opened neatly. As he sailed down silently in the quiet darkness all his instructions came clearly into his head, marshalled neatly and orderly, like soldiers in a line of march. He struck the ground with a breathtaking blow, then began applying them to the line-up of facts as they presented themselves. It was, he remembered, like following directions in a cookbook. Mix one grenade with one building. Run away. Hide. Move again. Stop. Crawl. Stir two grenades in that concrete tower. Dive for that ditch. Run for that wall. Into that barn. Wait. Wait for the sound of hell opening up on the beaches.

All went well for Stanley Wilson. Others had not been so lucky. He did what he had to do and joined an advancing unit . . . and now he was three thousand miles—and a long, long time—away from the coast of France. Each man who had survived had come back like an individual Columbus, to rediscover the world, a world that none had made—a world of confusion, uncertainty, frustration. Certainly not the world of peace and freedom that Stanley Wilson had fought so honestly for. Before, there had been uncertainty and confusion. But this would be cancelled out by one great master blow, a master blow which he gladly helped to deliver.

It didn't come off that way. The politicians in Washington, London and other free capitals of the world called on men like Stanley Wilson to go to the far reaches of the earth to die and bleed all over again to rectify their miscalculations. And Stanley Wilson, still the idealist with a head full of book sense, forgave the men in Washington, London and other capitals, and went to do his job. This time he was not so lucky . . . Now he was back again, and there still was no peace, and there was no wife named Elizabeth. Somewhere, on a distant and frozen hillside, he had left his flesh, his blood, his bones— and his ideals. And the shell that ruined his face and took away his leg had also deprived him of the possibility of ever having children of his own.

He finished shaving. And as he dismantled, cleaned and put away his razor, he caught a glimpse of his graying hair and his dull, disillusioned eyes. He hobbled to his easy chair and sat by the huge window, which was like a French window, that overlooked the busy street far beneath. He lay his crutches beside the chair, lighted a cigarette and blew smoke that billowed and drifted away and was lost in the expanse of the room. Elizabeth would be coming now to look after him, as she had done every day since he came home. A lump hardened in his stomach. *Goddam it! Why did she continue to pity him? Why wouldn't she leave him alone? Hadn't he told her he wanted to be left alone!*

"We want to be your friend, Lester and I both," she had almost pleaded. Lester! The guy with a head full of hard business sense, enough sense to stay home and get ahead in the world, the guy she had married. He wished now he hadn't torn her letter to a thousand pieces and thrown them toward the enemy lines. He'd like to read it over again in his present bitterness. It was an honest, simple, direct letter, not one of the usual "Dear John's," larded with cheap sentiment, self pity and phony excuses.

He sat very quiet, dreading to hear the doorbell. Today she was bringing the youngest child—little Lester. He would be about a year old now. Judy was two, and a beautiful little girl. She looked so much like Elizabeth. *I don't want her to come! Why doesn't she leave me alone! I don't need her pity. I don't need anybody!*

He picked up the paper from the arm of his chair. "UN TO HEAR NEW WORLD PEACE PLAN," said the headline. "DICTATOR THREATENS THREE MORE STATES," headed another story. "THREE THOUSAND FLEE SLAVE WORLD. PRESIDENT ASKS MORE APPROPRIATIONS FOR STRENGTHENING FORCES. NEW SPEED RECORD FOR JETS! CONGRESS PREDICTS HIGHER TAXES." And so it went. The paper was full of it. He flung it aside and swore.

For a few minutes he sat, thinking of nothing, or trying hard to think of nothing. A cloud passed over the sun and the room became dimmer. A cool breeze came in through the partially opened window. He shivered. He pulled himself up to close it. But instead he opened it wide, all the way.

He looked down at the street below. Down there people walked briskly, intent on their individual pursuits. They walked. He smiled sardonically. They all looked busy and important, as if each had his mission. He, too, had had a mission once. There was a young couple, arm in arm. Even from his great height, he could tell that they were young. He knew by the way they walked, close together. A little dog broke away from its mistress. The woman ran after it, caught up with it underneath a tree. Trees down there on the street . . . There had been trees down there beyond the beach, too. Was that the breeze that was stirring the trees, or waves lapping through the sky? Waves lapping through his life, through his heart

. . . The street grew dim, the people hazy. Was that the doorbell, or was it the captain's voice, ringing out an order? He pulled himself up in the window. Was that the coast of France stretching below?

"GERONIMO!"

THE LAST LIBERAL

JACOB GLUTZ was a Liberal. It could be said that he was an extreme, if not leftist, Liberal. In Saukberg, which is in the Rhineland, and as facts indicate overwhelmingly Christian-Democrat, he was the leading Liberal. Jacob took his Liberal leadership seriously. In defense of his inferior position, he did not like Christian-Democrats, and whenever he joined a crowd everybody knew what to expect. He came in slashing and whacking with his double-edged tongue. He represented strong, and what some people considered dangerous, thought in the small, isolated community.

Jacob Glutz was a tall, thin man, with long arms and hands like country hams. His head rested crookedly on a long neck, his lips were thin, his jaw awry, and his eyes were snapping and sharp. He was well armed with the past sins of the Christian-Democrats and kept abreast of their current misdeeds, and in his rasping but convincing voice could forcibly and luridly depict them. He always began a tirade with, "Those lousy Christian-Democrats!" And whenever the Bürgermeister of Saukberg passed by he would say with a little smile, "There goes one of those goddamn Christian-Democrats!"

But underneath it all Jacob Glutz and the Bürgermeister Potts were lifelong friends. The Bürgermeister, in direct contrast to Jacob, was a fat little man, whose round head sat closely on his thick shoulders. And he could harangue a crowd eloquently in his clear, melodious voice. Bürgermeister Potts was a politician who got results, attested to by his seemingly perpetual tenure in office. His political acumen warned him

THE LAST LIBERAL

107

that Jacob Glutz could become a powerful weight as a calamity to the Christian-Democratic Party in Saukberg. He suspected that Jacob was not yet aware of his potentialities, and the mayor determined to overhaul him before he woke up.

The Saukberg Wine Growers Association was about to have its annual election and it seemed a certainty Jacob Glutz would become its president. When that came about he would be in position to lead an organized revolt against the Christian-Democrats who had been in power for many years and there were growing murmurs of "time for a change" in the air. Moreover, Jacob knew where the Christian-Democrats had buried their long list of bodies. Nobody knew better than Bürgermeister Potts that if Jacob Glutz suddenly became aware of his political power he could turn not only the stomachs of the Wine Growers Association but those of some of the civic-minded Christian-Democratic Party members themselves. The Bürgermeister's crowd were shaking in their shoes.

One day Bürgermeister Potts went to Köln, and two days later he returned with a joyous, triumphant air. The next day, when the Saukberger *Zeitung* came out, everyone knew that Saukberg was going to have a new Rathaus. The old brick structure, which had stood for four-hundred years, was to be torn down and a modern stone building was to rise in its place. It would be a big construction job, financed out of the Christian-Democratic Party's treasury. There was happy talk about it.

But Jacob Glutz was not joyful. He was the only building contractor in the town, and everyone asked, "Jacob, are you going to build the new Christian-Democrat Rathaus?" Some of the party members, who had at one time or another been slashed by Jacob Glutz's harsh tongue, added, "It will be the biggest construction job since the Nazis ran the Autobahn through this district. There ought to be a nice profit in it."

The following week the Saukberger *Zeitung* announced that the job had been awarded to the Sagus Company, from Köln.

Next week this was denied, and there arose rumors. Instead of native stone the new building was to be constructed of imported Italian marble. It would cost much more than the original estimate. The Bürgermeister felt grieved, very grieved indeed, that he had to let the contract to an outsider. But, since the money was coming from the Christian-Democratic coffers, it would be impossible to award the work to one not of the party.

Jacob Glutz could not sleep. He went about with his head down and avoided everyone. This job would be the crowning feather in his cap, the biggest undertaking of his career, a testament to his life's work—a monument to Jacob Glutz! If he did not get the job he could not hold his head up in Saukberg ever. In the end he did what he knew he had to do.

He went to see Bürgermeister Potts at his home—after dark. The Bürgermeister appeared surprised to see him. "Ho, ho, Jacob Glutz!" he smiled. "Come into the library, Jacob. Have a cigar. Can I get you a cognac?"

"No, thank you, Albert," Jacob Glutz stammered. "You know well I don't smoke cigars, and I only drink beer." The Bürgermeister's casual attitude had put him ill at ease. He fumbled at his thin hair and twisted his Homburg in his great hands. "You know what brings me here, Albert," he managed to say. "I'm here about the contract."

The Bürgermeister feigned surprise. "What contract?"

"Come off it, Albert," the harassed contractor rasped, trying to smile. "The new Rathaus!"

The roly-poly little Bürgermeister rolled his fat round head and looked straight into his visitor's eyes. He intoned in amazement. "You, Jacob Glutz—a Liberal—and the worst kind at that, a leftist Liberal—expect me, a dyed-in-the-wool-old-line-Christian-Democrat to give you the contract for the new Rathaus, to be built with Christian-Democrats' money?"

Jacob crushed his Homburg, sweat ran down the furrows of his face, his eyes blinked. "Being the only contractor in

Saukberg . . . civic pride and all . . . I thought maybe we could forget politics this once."

The Bürgermeister folded his short arms over his round chest. "Jacob, it would be a public scandal! You! Saukberg's most blasphemous and extreme Liberal! The party would throw me out!" He paused while Jacob sweat and destroyed his Homburg. In a calmer tone he continued. "I realize, Jacob, how it must pain you to see this job go to a contractor in another town. But I can't do anything about it—unless—but no, that wouldn't work. Not with you, Jacob!"

Jacob Glutz was silent for a moment. When he spoke it was in the hollow voice of a man already doomed. "What wouldn't work, Albert?"

The Bürgermeister advanced a little, said coldly and resolutely, "The contract must go to a Christian-Democrat!"

Jacob momentarily envisioned greatness for himself. He saw, in a flash, the new Rathaus gleaming in the sun, tall and imposing, a lasting monument. And the thought of the handsome profit he would make on the job. "But, Albert, you know that's impossible. I'm a known Liberal. How could I . . . ?"

"Quite simple, Jacob," the confident little Bürgermeister said. Then he drove home his scheme. "Tomorrow night the Saukberg Wine Growers Association will choose a new president. That man will undoubtedly be you. Then you will be called upon to make a speech. At that time you will denounce the Liberals, atone for the long years of misguidance, apologize for the many evil things you have said about us in the past years. You will publicly become a Christian-Democrat."

Jacob Glutz groaned. "My God, Albert! In public, and after all these years as a known Liberal." Then he became all at once friendly. "Let me tell you something, Albert. It is true that all my life I have gone about, shall we say, belittling all kinds of Democrats, and sometimes—but jokingly—I have made remarks about our good Bürgermeister. But let me tell you what I did last election day. Was I around the polling places getting votes for the Liberals? No! I was out at old man Klein's place putting a new roof on his barn. I did not even vote! And the election before that, Albert. My poor brother's wife died in Amorbach and I drove all day to get there. And the election before that. I was busy laying the concrete for Paul Grusser's house and didn't take time off to go and vote. So you see, Albert, I have not been *against* the Democrats, really."

The Bürgermeister was not moved, but he spoke in an approving tone. "That is good, Jacob. That is good, what you tell me. Since you have not actually been a Liberal, it will not be difficult for you. I will be at the Wine Growers Association meeting tomorrow night, and right after you publicly become a Christian-Democrat I will put the contract in your hands."

Jacob Glutz built the new Rathaus, and it is there for all to see, a shining stone testament to the efficacy of the Christian-Democratic Party, for which Jacob votes every election.

But generations hence, when it is pulled down to make way for the edifice of some other party, in its cornerstone will be found the following litter representing a modern democracy: photographs of the Christian-Democratic Party head, photographs of other big-wig Democrats of this era, and Bürgermeister Albert Potts; several copies of the Saukberger *Zeitung;* a hundred D-mark note, a fifty, a twenty, a ten and several coins; and a liter of the local wine. And among these things will be found a brown piece of paper on which is inscribed in Jacob Glutz's handwriting: "This Building Is Hereby Dedicated to Saukberg's Last Liberal."

MY WONDERFUL HOME TOWN

I WAS BACK AGAIN—at last! I was glad I had arrived on the early morning train, before the town was awake. I could wander the streets alone, drink in the scenes, let my heart beat with the pure joy of being home again. Of course, I was anxious to see old friends; but the town came first. It was Sunday, a day of repose in the mid-South, and a lovely day. A bright June sun smiled down obliquely from a clear blue sky. It was a lovely day, indeed, after those long years of war in far-away places. I threw my duffle bag in the corner of the station waiting room and went out to greet my wonderful home town.

As I walked up the street from the depot to Courthouse Square my heart burned with happy rememoration. There was the Coca-Cola Plant, just as I had kept it in my mind all these years, its immaculate bottling machines shining behind the glass front. And there was the old Ice House. It too was the same; but its frame building looked worn and tired, like an old faithful darky bending low at the end of a long day's toil. What's that new building on the corner? Used to be a junk yard there. As I passed, I saw a sign, outlined in colored neon tubes: BEN GREEN & SON, METALS. I recalled Ben Green as a poor junk dealer, operating out of his hip pocket before the war.

When I came in view of the courthouse, a shadow passed over my heart. In my memory it had been huge and Gothic and imposing and gleaming. How small it seemed! And what a messy sight. The courtyard was littered with pop and beer bottles, papers and the usual trash left in the wake of a crowd. A temporary platform had been erected on the lawn and over it was a bunting banner, sagging in the middle, which urged: Vote for AUBREY HIGGINS for Governor! I had known Aubrey Higgins all his life. We used to play together, learned our ABC's in the same class, joined the army together. I went overseas and he served out World War II as some kind of official in the Ordnance Plant in Memphis, and came out with the rank of major. When it came time to go and fight again, however, he was busy running the town and raising a family.

I took a walk around the square. It had taken on a new face, a standard, modern face. Gone were the old leaded-glass windows from the store fronts, gone was the old WCTU iron watering trough that used to stand at the main entrance of the courthouse; though not in use for many years, it had been a familiar landmark. Store fronts all had broad expanses of polished plate glass display windows; the paved streets were white-lined for parking and each space was guarded over by a steel parking meter rising out of the concrete sidewalk. The old laced-iron balcony which once fringed the Dixie Hotel was also gone. The building had had a complete overhaul and looked just like hundreds of others to be seen in towns throughout the land. It even had a new name: SUGGS HOTEL. Every scene I looked on shattered my dreams. I was becoming afraid. I thought of the church I had belonged to ever since I could remember; surely that would not be changed. I crossed the street and walked rapidly toward it, a block from the square.

There it was, as it always had been—unaltered and as enduring as Time! It was a friendly building, a low brick structure painted white with a red roof. As I approached it I seemed to be walking back into my youth. Youth? I hadn't thought of that for a long time. What had happened to my youth? Oh, yes, I remember. I left part of it on the shores and in the fields of Europe, a long, long time ago, and the rest of it I had flung away on frozen and bloody Asian hillsides. I sat down on the concrete steps of the church and tried to gather myself, to soften the blow my homecoming had dealt me. The world had not stood still, I told myself. I should not have expected it to. Things change. They've got to. Businessmen and politicians call it progress. Progress? Yes, maybe that's what I've been fighting for—world progress.

The church seemed dwarfed somehow. Then I became conscious of another change. The new building across the street. It was the biggest one in town, five storeys, the new bank building. The corner where it stood used to be a vacant lot, where as a small boy I ran and played with Aubrey Higgins and the other children of the town; and beyond it had been my father's machine shop—God rest his harried soul; he like my mother had died too young.

While I sat there trying to reconcile my dreams of the old town with the shock of the new one, the events of another June morning came into my memory. That was a Sunday, too, and the events of that day long, long ago came to me in all their stark, horrible reality. My part of it had begun here, at the church . . .

I am sitting on a high-back varnished bench, looking down at my shoes and hearing the preacher's voice, a hollow, sad voice. I am not listening to what he is saying but *how* he is saying it: he sounds like he knows nobody believes what he is telling them and is mad at them because they do not. I can hear the birds singing and chirping outside in the chestnut trees, and I think they are singing because they are free and can stay outside and sing in the bright spring sunshine instead of having to listen to the preacher. My shoes pinch my feet and I will be glad when the sermon is over so I can take them off and run in my bare feet. On my last birthday I became eight years old and to please my mother was baptized; and am now obliged to stay in church after Sunday school and sit through the sermon.

Suddenly I hear people outside, hurrying past the open door behind me going toward Courthouse Square. They are running and talking in loud excited voices. A man says, "They got 'im! This time for sure they got the black bastard!" I know what is up; so does everybody else in the church. Some of the people are craning their necks toward the door, trying to see what is going on outside. Two men sitting near the door look grimly at each other, nod, get up and slip out.

Aubrey Higgins nudges me and whispers, "They got the nigger! Come on, let's go!" He takes me by the hand and the next thing I know I am tip-toeing down the green-carpeted aisle, feeling the preacher's eyes in the middle of my back, as his voice goes up louder and querulous. Aubrey is two years older than I am—he is ten—and is leading the way, and I think how lucky he is because the preacher's eyes are not on his back. We finally get to the door, skip down the steps and fly toward Courthouse Square.

A large knot of men have assembled on the courthouse lawn and others are coming from all directions. One man, who seems to be taking charge, has a coil of rope on his arm. As Aubrey and I come closer we can hear what he is saying. "We'll use this! It's seagrass rope. It'll take the skin off his neck before it kills 'im. I kicked in the door of the Forked Deer Hardware Store and took it." He grins and I can see there is something frightening in his face.

I stop, and Aubrey tries to pull me along by the arm. "Come on!" he urges. "Let's get a look at the nigger."

"Aw, I bet they haven't got him," I protest, scared and excited. "My dad says that man's clear out of the county by now. Besides, I'm hungry. I'm going home and get something to eat. I—I'll come back and see the hanging, if they've really got him."

"You can't go home now!" Aubrey says, like he is peeved at me. " 'Course they got 'im. Come on, let's see!" He sweeps me along toward the crowd.

I am afraid they have got the man, and I don't want to see him. I am afraid of the look on the faces of the men in the crowd. They have been after the Negro for more than a week now and there have been daily rumors that he has been caught —in Clarksville, in Nashville, in Tupelo below the state line. From the stir and tempo of things I begin to believe they really have got him this time. Aubrey pushes me into the crowd and I am getting excited and begin to be not so much afraid. I forget all about my tight shoes now. "Where is he? Who's got him?" demands the man with the rope.

There is a milling, and a loosening up of the crowd. A low grumbling arises and some of the men begin cursing loudly. A little man with a high celluloid collar and tobacco juice in the corners of his mouth reassures them. "They got 'im, all right!" he snarls. "I seen 'em bringin' 'im in, in a car. They caught 'im on the railroad tracks down near Memphis."

"I bet they took the black sonuvabitch to the jail," complains the rope man. "Come on! We'll go get 'im!" With the coiled rope on his shoulders as his badge of authority, he leads the mob off in the direction of the jail.

Resembling a large black tadpole, the rabble wriggles up the street toward the jail, which is a block from the courthouse in the other direction from my church. Aubrey pulls me along, trying to keep up with the rope man, who is leading the mob. I break away and linger back, and just when the tadpole flattens its blunt head against the front of the jailhouse, I become frightened and ashamed and dart down an alley and come out on the next street. I am thinking that my mother will be very angry with me because I left church, and I decide to go back and slip quietly in again. Then I see the Negro. His hands are cuffed behind his back and he is being hustled along by four men with fierce, wild expressions in their faces. I get a good look at him. He is a small man, wiry and thin; he has black, curly short hair and it is combed neatly and is parted on one side. His nose is straight, not flat and flared, and he has a high forehead, like a white man's; but he is yellow.

The little group are upon me before I can run away, and I

am looking straight into the Negro's eyes. If I live to be a hundred and thirty years old I will never be able to forget that man's eyes. They are thrown wide with fear and their brown pupils glisten in the sun. They are rolled so that all of the whites are showing. (I have seen such eyes many times since—on the coasts and in the fields of Europe and on the cold hills of Asia. They are the eyes that see Death.) The man's legs are rigid, and the men are shoving him along, forcing one leg before the other as if he is drunk or paralyzed. But he is neither drunk nor paralyzed; he is just scared stiff.

I cannot go back to church now and I cannot run away. Seeing the man has done something to me. I am not afraid any more. I have a strange unreasoning feeling that he needs me. I cannot help him and I cannot leave him. So I follow as closely as I can to the man. I feel friendly toward him; maybe I will get a chance to touch him. The men drag him to the courthouse and up the concrete steps and hustle him into the County Court Clerk's office, after smashing down the door. There are other rooms but this is the handiest one. "Why waste time on a trial?" one of the men asks. "We know he's guilty as all hell."

"This ain't gonna take long," says another, and he hits the man in the face with his fist, knocking him in a chair.

By now men are pouring in through all four of the courthouse's doors. Word has got around that they have the Negro here. They jam into the County Court Clerk's office until it is full and overflowing. I am pressed into a corner, but I can still see the Negro in the chair. He is breathing heavily and his eyes are still open wide. I wish I could let him know I am still here.

"Nigger, we're giving you a trial," somebody says. "Do you understand? You're gettin' a fair trial. Now all you gotta do is confess."

"Yeah, nigger! 'Fess up!" a louder voice yells. "You done it, didn't you, nigger! We know you done it. You're the nigger we're lookin' for, ain't you? You're the one that raped her, ain't you?"

"He's the nigger, all right!" cries another man. "He's a yeller nigger, and there ain't no yeller nigger no good. What are we wastin' time fer? Come on, let's do what we got to do and git it over with."

"Speak up, nigger!" demands the first man. "Say you're the nigger we want and that you done it!"

" 'Course he done it! He's a yeller nigger, ain't he?"

A crash of fist on flesh. "You black sonuvabitch! You done it, didn't you?" Another crash and I shut my eyes.

There is a low moaning and the man is trying to say something. "What's he sayin'?" growls the second man. "What's the yeller bastard sayin'?"

The first man is leaning close to the Negro's head, his fist doubled up. He straightens up, glares at the crowd. "The sonuvabitch says he ain't the nigger."

" 'Course he is! We gotta hang 'im! What we wastin' time fer?"

"What's the verdict, men?" shouts the first man.

"Guilty!" "Guilty!" "Guilty!" "The yeller sonuvabitch is guilty as hell!"

"Take 'im away!"

The man is snatched up from the chair and pushed toward the door through the crowd. When they get him outside, the man with the rope runs up and tries to take charge. He begins to unwind his rope. "That poplar tree in the southwest corner. We'll string 'im up there."

"Keep your shirt on," growls one of the men who is holding onto the Negro. "We got other ideas."

"What you goin' to do?" asks the rope man.

"We're goin' to teach this goddamn nigger a lesson good. He tried to lie out of it. We're goin' to burn the black sonuvabitch!"

"Burn 'im!" "Burn 'im!" It strikes through the mob like a

charge of violently dancing electricity. A roar of approval goes up and fresh energy strikes into the crowd, and it takes on new impetus. Now it is truly a mob. The big black tadpole is now a monstrous beast, vicious and deadly. "Bring 'im to the vacant lot!" the rope man shouts, and leads the way.

I try to keep close to the man, am pushed and shoved and knocked down, and once or twice I am in danger of being trampled badly, I get up, fall, push, crawl, am carried along by angry flying legs and feet. Always I try to keep close enough to see the man who is limp now; and as he is dragged help-lessly along his toes trace two small furrows in the soft spring grass. "We need a stake!" somebody shouts. "Get a stake!"

Half a dozen men detach themselves from the mob and fall wildly upon a buckboard which is standing, with a horse be-tween its shafts, by the WCTU watering trough. In no time, off come two wheels and an axle is torn out. Holding the axle over their heads the men fairly run back to the mob shouting, "We got a stake! We got a stake!"

"We need a sledgehammer!" And several men dash toward my father's machine shop. I know they will smash down the door, like they did at the county clerk's office, but there is nothing I can do. I must stay close to the man. In a few minutes the men appear, holding the big hammer over their heads, working their way through the mob to the men with the axle.

As they drive the stake in the ground, a heavy silence hangs over the lot. The sledgehammer resounds on the steel axle with sickening, melancholy blows. In the hush I can hear the faint echo of my preacher's voice floating out the open door of the church down the street. It rises and falls hollowly and with a pathetic futility. The pounding ceases and the noise of the mob rises once more. I see a little path opening up through the press of people, and up it comes; one, two, three, four men holding long iron rods in the air. The ends are white-hot. They are coming from my father's machine shop, and now I understand the red sparks shooting out of the chimney; they have had the blower furnace going. "No! No!" I cry, and try to fight my way to the Negro man, who has now been stripped naked and is lashed to the stake with telephone wire. Above the heads of everybody I can see the red-hot iron rods—one, two, three, four—moving closer to the center of the mob. I can see the man. He sees the red-hot rods coming. He thrashes about, throwing himself madly against the wires, which cut into his body. He turns his head round, looking—looking with his wild frightful eyes. I want to shout out, "Here! Here I am!"

The rods reach the center of the mob, halt. There is another dead, awful silence; and the voice of the preacher can be heard again, faintly, futilely. One by one the red-hot irons are lowered. A moment later the Negro's terrified voice rends the air. It is deafening, horrible, pitiful—the cry of a human, the wail of an animal. "O-OHOOO! Lawd! Lawd! Lawdy!" It rings out loud and penetrating. My heart stops beating, a feeling of cold scales passes up the backs of my legs, and I bite my lip until the blood runs down my chin.

Another cry, prolonged and piercing. Another and another. Then great, supplicating sobs. Soon it ceases entirely, and I know the man is beyond their torture now. He does not need me any more and I work my way out of the mob. A few minutes later, tall flames begin to leap up from the center of the lot. They are bringing more cans of gasoline as I walk toward the church. Services are over and the people are coming out; there is hardly a handful, because most of the men had left to join the mob. Then I come upon Aubrey. He is wild-eyed and excited. "Where'd you go?" he says breathlessly. "Did you see the nigger! Look, I got a souvenir!" He holds up a swatch of blue chambray cloth. "It's part of his shirt. I sure had a fight to get it."

. . . The bells in the church belfry suddenly clanged out, loud and long and pealing, bringing me back to the present.

Soon people would be coming to church; if I remained here I could see old friends. Although my parents both had been dead a long time and I had no relatives here, there would be a few old friends left. Quite abruptly I realized I was afraid to see them; in fact, I was anxious not to see any of them. Certainly they would each have a new façade, like the town itself, but I was afraid of what I would find underneath. I did not wish to witness a display of their base vanities, stupid pretenses and vile hypocrisies. I would see their minds as servile, covetous, arrogant, grasping and bigoted. Suddenly I found myself going rapidly toward the depot. I hardly gave a passing glance to the shining establishment of Ben Green & Son, the old Ice House or the Coca-Cola Plant. I snatched up my duffle bag and boarded the very next train. Standing on the observation platform, I watched the little town fall away in the distance; and then I began to remember my wonderful home town as I had come to dream of it.

THE RAKE AND THE HAYRAKE

When P. T. Lamont, my editor, practically shanghaied me aboard a plane bound for Germany to get what he called the "true color of the Rhineland" for a serial I was writing, I expected to return within a month, perhaps a fortnight. At any rate I was determined to get back as soon as possible. For I was one of those confirmed New Yorkers who believes steadfastly that all the world revolves around the metropolis of New York City. And I had no intention of spending any more of my days than I was forced to away from its wonderful stone cliffs and fascinating little caves. Besides there was Clarisse.

Lovely, devoted, Clarisse Fontaine! Each time we said goodbye I cut my banishment shorter. When we said it—a long touching farewell—in her dressing room, her large dark eyes were filled and about to spill over. We repeated this performance, but more fully and with far more satisfaction, in the privacy of her apartment, and as she tied my Windsor (I never could manage one of those fool things), large tears were in her ivory, shadowy cheeks. I kissed her splendid red lips, she smiled, and her brilliant teeth outshone her bright smile. "Darling, I won't live until you are back and I am in your arms again!"

We said goodbye briefly at the bar in the Stork Club, and at El Morocco, and at our favorite little bar down on Fifty-eighth. With each goodbye I promised to come back sooner. By the time we said goodbye at the airport I was sure that upon my return I would make good my long-standing promises to marry the lovely musical comedy star. Yes, I had wasted enough time. After all, I thought, I owed Clarisse a lot. Hadn't she devoted everything to me: trust, love, constancy— and herself. I had always prided myself on being neither a gentleman nor a sentimentalist. In fact, I was known around Broadway as something of a rake. Nevertheless, I knew a good thing when I saw one, and Clarisse was the best in my existence. Clarisse was the metropolis itself: she was bustling Broadway, smart Fifth Avenue, glamorous Times Square, she was the slender, tall, inspiring towers of Manhattan. And I loved them all. Marrying Clarisse would be like eating my cake and having it, too. When I got this job done and landed back in New York, I'd be a different guy. Yes, indeed!

Perhaps dame Fate didn't like my sudden turnabout. Maybe that's why she threw Magda and the old fashioned hayrake at me.

When I stepped off the local *Rheinufer* train into the jaundiced spring sunlight, Professor Wilhelm Brandt was standing on the stone platform waiting for me, as P. T. had assured me he would be. The retired professor had a villa on the Rhine, in a similar locale to that which I was creating for my story. The old *Bürger* belied his seventy-odd years. In spite of his snow-white hair his light blue eyes were keen and clear. Nowhere was his face slack and lined. The skin was wrinkled only around the eyes, and was reddened by long walks in the sun (with his pretty niece, Magda, I was to learn later). He smiled a healthy smile and made a little erect bow, bending only his powerful, straight back. He extended me a hearty hand, said in good English, "Welcome to Germany, my son."

Without waiting to be prompted by the elder male, as most *Mädchen* would have done, Magda stepped forward. "I'm Magda Westermann," she said in her clear low-pitched voice.

I noticed that she was not thick through the middle, as some of the returning occupation veterans had assured me Fräuleins were, but that her waist was extremely narrow. Or did it just seem narrow because of her abundant high bosom?

"P. T. didn't tell me about you," was all I could think of to say.

She turned her eyes full upon me. They were wide and bold and slate-colored. I tried to avoid their seductive lure by concentrating on the three freckles making faint shadows on her small nose. She smiled. "I suppose not," she said. "He didn't know me. I was in school in England when he was here."

Magda drove the convertible. I sat in front with her. Professor Brandt rode in back with my bags. As we passed through fields of vivid green grass among which tall yellow dandelions rose up like shafts of yellow light, and wound through rolling hills that seemed to be walking gently up to the bank of the Rhine, I had to admit that P. T. had the right idea. Already descriptive words and phrases were haunting my mind. I would be back in my wonderful New York in no time—and in my Clarisse's arms.

Magda turned the car sharply, careening me toward her. Something inside me stirred. She looked at me and smiled, her red lips parting to reveal even white teeth. I saw that she was aware of what she could do to me, and I prompted my susceptible heart to post "Danger, girl at work!" signs to comfort every tingling nerve of my body. And I silently repeated my promises to Clarisse to hurry back to New York.

Professor Brandt and his niece posited me comfortably, in truly Old World style. The Brandt villa (I have not to this day made up my mind whether it is a small castle or a large villa) nestles on what could be considered an extremely large hill or a small mountain, high above the Rhine. I had a large suite on the second floor with a shaded balcony which overlooked the wide, slow-moving river, as seen through tall pines whose branches, like uplifted arms, twinkled with singing birds. I plunged into my work with great industry. The old professor was helpful with history, folklore and tips on "where to find it." Magda was always usefully near me but never intrusive. Among the many little comforts she provided me with was *ein Kännchen Kaffee* continually at my elbow. In moments of relaxation I caught myself reflecting on the splendid domestic virtues of the Continental woman, as compared to those of the mundane cliff-dwelling female of New York City.

My work went well and I began to look forward to putting these singing birds, this clean sky and wholesome scenery behind me and flying back to Clarisse and New York's dingy, smoke-filled—but ever so familiar and intimate—night clubs and cafes.

Every day Magda drove me into the little town at the foot of the mountain and helped me dig through the musty library files. Whenever I got stuck with my clumsy "New York U" brand of *Deutsch* she was sweetly helpful. One day as we left the library I suggested that we stay in town for dinner. My work was nearly finished and I was in an expansive mood. Magda was delighted, said she knew just the place. Taking me by the hand she led me down narrow cobblestone streets, where white stucco houses whose walls were crisscrossed with brown-hued logs protruded their upper storeys toward each other like shy, dressed-up lovers. We passed through a wooded park where the willows, crowding over the path from both sides, brought us very close together and my knee touched again and again Magda's lithe but delicately yielding leg.

At last we reached the cafe, a low age-stained sandstone building. Magda told me it was famous because Napoleon once spent a fortnight there and had a brief but inflammatory romance with the innkeeper's niece. Before dinner we had a bottle of *Liebfrauenmilch* wine, which gently and lovingly put a golden hue on the face of the world. Magda's eyes seemed larger and bluer, her skin glowing, her lips redder and warmer. Her hair was a rich, smooth chestnut; her voice was liquid silver.

After dinner we took a stroll along the river, and I found myself singing praises of *schönes Deutschland.*

"Look!" cried Magda, pointing to the wharf below us. "The *Fee Königin!* It goes up the river every night during the summer months."

The little excursion boat was painted white and gaily decorated, ready to sail. It resembled a prim coquette, awaiting with a cavalier air her admirers.

The trip was calm and romantic. Everywhere, all around us, were lovers under a starry and warm sky. A trio of musicians played stringed instruments, while boy and girl, pressed to one another, became lost in the emotion of desire, in the excitement of promised bliss. The warm darkness seemed full of floating kisses. A sensation of tenderness made the air languishing and stifling. All those embracing people, intoxicated with the same intention, the same thought, roused a fever in me. There was a look in Magda's slate-blue eyes that contained an appeal and a response, a desire and an avowal. My arm slipped around her waist. An unexpected wave rocked the boat, pulling me away from her. Then I realized my danger. And I concentrated on Clarisse and New York. The spell appeared broken.

We drove back home in silence. Magda kept her eyes on the road ahead. I wondered what she was thinking. I hoped not the same thing I was thinking!

When I was undressed and about to go to bed there was a rap on my door. I opened it to see Magda, also ready for bed. She carried an armful of books, which she dumped into my hands. There was Freud, Jung, Adler, Krafft-Ebing. Her eyes were half-mocking, half-promising, wholly fascinating. "Books!" she said petulantly. "Something for you to read before going to sleep." She was gone.

I stood staring dumbly after her, breathing her perfume and seeing the exquisite picture she made in her delicate blue negligee, and I realized again my danger. I knew what a wonderful book of romance *she* could be. I knew, too, that I would be turning a few pages soon unless I hastened back to New York and my sophisticated Clarisse.

Early next morning I appeared downstairs with folded typewriter, bulging briefcase and packed bags. Professor Brandt was shocked. He strongly insisted that I postpone my departure for at least another day. A special dinner was being prepared for me that night. *"Rheinlachs* and *Eisbombe,"* he boomed, heaving his big chest and smiling. I cast a reassuring glance at my packed bags, and since Magda was not present, I sanely reasoned that the crisis had been passed, and so consented.

Dinner was over early and Magda asked if I'd like to take a drive. Fortified with confidence, for all day long I had filled my mind with Clarisse and ambitious plans for parties and night club catching-up when I reached New York, I said I would like to see the sunset from across the Rhine once again before I left.

Magda drove down the narrow dirt road, wide enough only for a single vehicle, toward the river. The dying sun caused the whole sky to glow, and the high ridge of the river bank in front of us arched its back in a dark mass against the blazing horizon like a giant struggling in a conflagration. The road, never widening, wound on to the foot of this giant, then rose straight up. At the top Magda stopped her car.

Below us lay the broad, lazy Rhine, with the low sun painting long yellow shafts across its shimmering surface. We watched this wonderful scene in silence. For the first time in weeks I was enjoying complete relaxation—my mind at ease. My work was done, and a satisfying job, too. No words, no phrases, no fitful fancies tumbled about in my head. I was enjoyably free . . .

Magda stood close beside me. The fragrance of her permeated my senses. The nearness of her brought me tremblingly alive. I drew her close in my arms and her slender body melted into mine. My lips found hers, tender and seeking as I had known they would be. A long kiss . . . holding all that was beautiful, promising all that I had desired in life. She opened her eyes and I saw what they said: *When you will.* An incandescent explosion occurred, in slow motion, in my breast. I pushed her away.

"We'd better start back," I said hoarsely.

Magda was silent for a moment, then she said, "Of course," and climbed in the car.

Coming round the sharp curve at the bottom of the ascent, Magda suddenly braked the car. Then I saw the hayrake, its great wheels turning slowly in the little gullies on each side of the road. Between its wheels, mounted on its wide axle, was its rack of great curved steel teeth, like a giant hand. It was drawn by two thick-rumped horses plodding slowly, content that the day's work was done. The farmer seated behind the horses glanced over his shoulder at us, made a hopeless gesture. At once I saw there absolutely was no way of passing this contraption, of getting around it. We would have to wait for it to turn off the lane whenever it came to a crossroad. Magda got it too—and more. She switched off the motor and looked at me. She was laughing softly, intoxication in every line of her. Behind us, far out across the river, the sun slipped down into the hills, and the slowly gathering gloom witnessed my surrender.

It was pitch dark before we were ready to go. With Magda's help I finally got the Windsor back in my tie, and she started the car, turned on the lights and we headed for home.

But it didn't end as Magda had planned it. While she no doubt knew her Freud and Jung and Adler and Krafft-Ebing, she didn't know me. She didn't know that I'm neither a sentimentalist nor a gentleman; she didn't know what a rake I really am. I got up early the next morning, before the household was awake, grabbed my bags and left.

Only occasionally have I ever uttered Magda's name since. It happens sometimes, in rare moments of close ecstasy with my wife Clarisse, after which she always demands a lot of explaining. I ought to tell her, I suppose, about Magda and the hayrake. But, as I said, I'm something of a rake myself.

FURY OVER THE HIMALAYAS

THE COLD FOG, settling like an immense shroud over the air base at Kunming, had driven everyone indoors except the mechanics and field attendants who, resolute in their duties and oblivious to discomfort, were about the business of refueling and checking my plane.

Night had fallen under a queer sky. The sun, pale and without rays and pouring down a strangely indecisive light, had dropped sickly down behind a dense black cloud which resembled a solid object as formidable as the great mountain upon which it was couched. Anxious about the impending weather, I had remained outside, eyes clamped upon that motionless bank of clouds with sinister and ominous tint; for, before the passing of midnight, I must fly over and beyond the towering Himalaya Range to Chabua in Assam Province, India. And propped upon the monstrous shoulders of that hump of earth and stone was the storm center, threatening and defiant, as if to wilt my courage. Sprawled over a darkening sky were big, lurid stars. And while I watched, the whole lot took flight together, leaving a blackness like something palpable, something you could reach out and lay hands on. And rapidly there was a lowering of the darkness, as if the hooded lanterns of all the Orient were turned down.

I went into the Pilots' Lounge, where a group of my fellow officers were gathered, some playing poker, some catching a bit of sleep before their call, others engaged in nostalgic talk about girls and home—home far away in safe and comfortable America. I could not inject my thoughts into the affairs of any of the groups, so I wandered from quarter to quarter anxiously paying out the time, smoking cigarettes end on end. Then suddenly, as I expected, it came booming over the loudspeaker.

"Captain Hull! Captain George Hull!"

When I got to the plane Lt. Leo Reilly and Sgt. Wai Lee, a Chinese boy, were waiting for me, flying togs donned. Lt. Reilly was my co-pilot and Sgt. Wai Lee was to be my radioman. It was quickly decided that we would fly the north route. The storm formation over The Hump had not begun to move. It was still crouched, full of purpose, on that lofty, gray summit. When it moved it would veer south. It usually did, and, banking on its customary behavior, we hoped to elude it. Though the last pilot in had reported a sleet storm blowing at fifteen thousand feet in the vicinity of Lake Tali, on the northern course, I elected to chance that route, flying above the sleet, rather than hazard going through the cloud formation.

We took off amid a great convulsion of fog that roamed the field like hordes of whimsical, fluid tumbleweed, allowing only dismal in-and-out visibility. I gave the Linda Sue, which was the affectionate name I had given my plane and which Lt. Reilly had carefully painted on each side of its nose, full throttles and it swept down the strip, lifted its wheels into the night air and folded them stiffly up and into the wing-wells. At once we were on instruments. Solely by the gauges I labored the Linda Sue up and up through the pallid fog. Lt. Reilly—he was a lanky, hollow-cheeked Georgian, and when he smiled, which was almost constantly, tiny crinkles fanned out from his eyes giving radiance to the twinkle therein—made an indistinct remark: "Nasty stuff, this old fog . . ."

At fifteen thousand feet, instead of the mist clearing as we had counted on, it became thicker and the turbulence increased, tossing, jerking, lurching the plane. At eighteen thousand the situation grew worse. Reilly and Wai Lee looked at me anxiously through the big round lenses of their goggles and above their dog-nosed oxygen masks and it struck me that the three of us, peering into the ever thickening vapor through our queer headgear, looked like weird creatures from another planet. In a brilliant burst of lightning we saw great furls of clouds boiling and writhing, and enveloping us. Then the truth, with profound clarity, clamped down—the storm had caught us. It had moved north instead of south. And now, like a living thing, it was slyly and wrathfully waylaying us. Already in its clutches, I had no choice but to accept its challenge, to grapple with it, to wrestle it.

Like the sudden bursting of a drum of fury it exploded round us with an overpowering concussion. Compressed wrath unleashed itself and beat the Linda Sue with hate, clawed, twisted and bent her slender wings like a personal enemy. Her engines roared out against this abuse, and there was the throb like the chant of a trampling multitude. Reilly leaned over and, lowering his mask, shouted above the drumming of the storm: "We're sure in for it now, Cap'n!"

The airspeed indicator wound backward and forward like a runaway clock: the rate-of-climb shot up and down crazily, measuring off hundreds of feet ascent and descent in quick alternation: the ball-and-bank quivered, jiggled and behaved madly: the radio crackled, buzzed and squealed in my ears until I flung off my headset, giving it up as absolutely useless.

The rain came as a vicious onrushing of unchained fury. The gale and the water lashed us from all sides. There was contempt in the pounding, rage in the blows that fell. The Linda Sue lunged, tossed, plunged, shuddered and quivered, staking her life against this hard tumbling. She rumbled deep in her innards, and I wondered if she were ready to turn over on her back and give up to the violence of the storm. She was like a derelict, caught in the path of a routed, raging army. Hustled terribly, trampled on, borne up, flung wildly. I began to doubt that our stout, sleek Linda Sue would live through it.

With this new violence I was anxious not to get muddled

and lose control of the plane, so I abandoned all reference to its course, because the compass swung far both ways, wriggling in its pivot, and sometimes whirled so that it was unreadable. Fixing all my attention on the airspeed indicator, I sought, against all its wild oscillation, to keep it as constant as possible. The important thing was to keep the plane flying, and it must hold together: if I let it pick up too much speed it would disintegrate under the larruping of the storm, and if I pulled the nose too high, stalling it, it would succumb instantly to the gale and be snapped into an uncontrollable spin. I had throttled back, easing the strain, when we first sliced into the devilish thermals which shot us skywards for thousands of feet at breathtaking speed and then suddenly jerked us down like a falling meteor.

I know there are in a pilot's experiences unexpected, often irrational, notions, moments when irrelevant but sometimes significant thoughts strike across the trouble reason. With the storm striving to rout the very spirit out of the plane, the winds tugging and wrenching its delicate, thin-veined wings, and the rain beating it with unbound ferocity, I envisioned the tempest as a personal opponent. It was, in my violent whim, as a contest between two wrestlers, no rules recognized, no holds barred—a contest in which I knew I was bested. And, oddly, I thought of David and Goliath. David had a slingshot. I had my airspeed indicator.

In the raging Erebus outside, St. Elmo's fire encircled the paths of the two propellers like weird twin-hoops out of hell's own inferno. It pirouetted and darted along the leading edges of the wings, out around their tips, and continued its diabolic antics back into the cockpit itself. In little bluish-yellow tongues of unbottled fire it licked the metal-studded instrument panel at will, (As I understood St. Elmo's fire, it was a phenomenon caused by the sudden releasing of positive and negative electrical currents gathered from the storm, harnessed in raindrops and then released when the charged drops were demolished against the metal surfaces of the plane.) Violently snatched up or down as if by the hand of a devil, the plane would suddenly and momentarily leave the St. Elmo's fire behind, like the trailing flames from a plummeting ball of brimstone. The vivid and frequent bolts of lightning effaced it momentarily, giving short respite from its ghostly propinquity. In spite of the added danger of the increasing violence of the lightning, I was glad when a bolt of it illuminated the heavens, for in that short interim was my only chance of seeing a mountain peak that might loom in our path.

Lt. Reilly leaned over, indicated the oxygen gauge, and yelled out the side of his mask: "Cap'n, it'll soon be gone, what with three of us drawin' off'n it." My decision had to be instantaneous. I motioned Wai Lee forward—as radio operator he was perfectly useless to us now, for the electricity in the storm had rendered radio equipment valueless—he lowered his head between Reilly and myself, and I felt the cold metal ring of his dog-nosed oxygen gear against my cheek as he calmly awaited orders. I told him: "Turn off your oxygen and remove your mask." Immediately and without compunction he obeyed, and when I saw his calm, blank and gentle face, like the face of a blind man, I knew, for the first time in my life, the painful burden of command. The humbleness I felt in the face of that Chinese youth's tranquil valor purged me forever of all feeling of superiority over other human beings, turned me against caste, and resolved me to eternally rebel against the tyranny of command. Out of this fresh strange emotion I drew vigor, determination, new strength.

"How is it in back?"

He returned presently and told me the tin ingots were gnawing at their leashes. They were sure to break away from their beddings, he told me, if the plane kept up this wild lunging and plunging. This brought me up sharp. Tin ingots, each weighing one hundred and twenty pounds, knocking and tumbling about the frail Linda Sue's hull! They would snap the control cables like threads, smash the operational units like match boxes. Or they would come crashing forward as mad, living monsters, crushing the three of us. I shouted above the pounding of the storm for Wai Lee to keep me warned.

"God Almighty!" shouted Reilly. "That'll finish us off for sure!" I saw it at the same time, in the light of a sustained quivering shaft of lightning. We were flying into a driving Niagara of sleet. Shoving the throttles fully open, I felt the engines surge and strain under their full measure of power. I increased the angle of climb and the Linda Sue bore her nose into the sleet bank at twenty thousand feet. This was a wet, sloppy ice, the kind that spreads and freezes over the surfaces, robbing you of altitude; not on account of the added weight but because the ice molds unevenly, changing the airfoil of the wings, thus diminishing their lifting efficiency. As the engines labored without intermission, thrusting the Linda Sue harshly on through the ice, a series of *ifs* beset me: If we were not blown into a mountain—if the engines did not give up—if the tin ingots did not break loose—if the plane held together against the tempest—and if the oxygen held out, then there was a chance of our coming through. Something within me seemed to turn over, bringing a feeling that we were done for.

Glancing at the oxygen gauge, I saw that the precious stuff would not hold out. I dropped my mask and drew Reilly close and told him: "We'll take it in shifts. Two minutes at a time, then switch." I left off my mask, giving him the first turn. This was nearly our undoing. For before I realized what was happening the windshield in front of me had completely frosted up on the inside. Enormously occupied, I was unaware of the intense cold, oblivious to my freezing feet. The feeble streams of warm air from the heater vents were doing their best but it wasn't enough; we were freezing. My warm moist breath released in the cockpit had produced the frosting effect of a refrigerator. The windshield had iced up on the inside and all contact with the outside world was shut off.

I motioned for Reilly to take over. "Keep the airspeed constant!" I yelled. Then I reached for something with which to remove the opaque coating, make a tiny hole at least. Throughout my pockets I found nothing. In desperation I drew off my fleece-lined glove and pressed my hand flat against the crusty ice. Slowly I felt the ice giving way to the heat from my palm. With my glove I cleared a small area about the size of the inside of my hand. To this I pressed one eye and waited for the first flash of lightning. It came in the shape of a huge, blazing Z. Through the boiling clouds unmistakably I saw it—the grey, imminent mountain. It towered to an altitude far above us and was directly on our nose. Screaming at Reilly, I jarred him loose from the controls, kicked hard left rudder and pulled the nose high in a climbing turn. The Linda Sue shuddered momentarily then rose slowly, staggeringly, as if she were lifting the mountain itself, her slender wings flexing to the breaking point under the immense strain. But she swept gently round, and, eye fastened on my small aperture, I stared aghast at the petrifying panorama. My spirits went tumbling and my heart rose to my throat. We were hemmed in by ugly, defiant mountain peaks. It was absolutely impossible to clear them.

There was a hand on my shoulder and I turned to peer into the pinched, blue-tinted face of Wai Lee. Without words he pointed aft. I turned in my seat harness, and my drooping spirits now plummeted. Sliding, lurching, tumbling over each other, pitching from side to side hammering about the cabin were the wild, unleashed ingots. I could expect no aid from anyone on earth. Yet, somehow, I did not give up—not quite. I turned my attention to the controls with the feeling of a defeated man, staggering from the field of battle; but somehow with the faint conviction that there was *something, something* still that might be done.

Then in the next instant the face of the whole world was changed. The scene cutting an arc across my tiny peephole sent my heart bounding. Through a luminous fissure in the dying storm a scant gorge appeared in the mountain range, and directly ahead.

I leveled out and headed straight for it. Though when it was too late to turn back I perceived that the narrow gap would not pass the Linda Sue with her enormous wing span. But I still had a chance, one small chance. I hauled back painstakingly on the wheel, drew it cautiously to the left, and with both my feet held hard top rudder. The Linda Sue heaved over on her side and, in this ungainly position, sliced into the little gap. With all my strength and nerves I held her in this unorthodox attitude while sending her torturously through the passage. Interminable moments dragged while sheer stone walls scraped by, winding, contracting, widening. Then the mountain walls fell away and there was a diminishing of the winds. I righted the Linda Sue, and a few amazing stars blinked at me through the breaks in the clouds.

Under a delightfully star-studded canopy and drenched in the brightest, gayest moonlight I ever did see, we sailed smoothly, nearing Assam. Reilly wore a smile you could see a mile. Wai Lee, having secured the recalcitrant ingots, stood calmly between us. Reilly pointed toward a moonlit village sleeping peacefully between the breasts of some gently rounded hills. "Shangri La," he said.

"Yes, Reilly," I smiled, "there are a lot of Shangri La's."

THE SUPERMAN

A friend returning from the Burma-India Theater after
World War II brought me the root idea for this piece in
the form of an old jungle folktale. The root idea is here,
yet by adapting it to a concept vital and tragic to the war,
I believe I have made a new thing of it.   J. W. B.

In the Upper Hukong Valley, under the mighty arms of the
Himalayas, there is a rectangular clearing which was once an
emergency landing strip. Into this man-made savannah, out
of the green jungle wall there came one day a Hillman whose
name was Drozak. Had this little native, who wore natural
bangs, had enormous feet, and was possessed of still, sunken
eyes, been so inclined he could have probed beneath the
whorls and loops of ever-juvenescent moss, vines, leaves and
ferns and found the rotting stretches of steel runway matting
that ran the entire length of the clearing. But that day the
heart of this gentle Hillman was heavy and his thoughts were
troubled.

Drozak was returning to his home beyond the giant moun-
tains bearing unhappy news for his father who, influenced by
the ravings of a half-mad missionary, had many, many moons
ago sent his only son out of the jungle to bring back knowledge of the missionary's far-off civilization. Returning, Drozak
must tell his father that these civilizations were not, as advertised by the lean, fiery-eyed, howling holy man, glowing
bright with virtue, but were false. He must report that the
glittering advantages of which the strange white man spoke
had not taught men to be wise or how to do things the right

way, and that most things in the world are done wrong. He must tell his father that men preached goodness but were not good; that they demanded tolerance of others but were intolerant themselves; made hurrahs for peace but planned wars; preached equality but practised many forms of slavery. He must tell of the helplessness of men in these far-off civilizations beyond the jungle. He must affirm that the law of the jungle was indeed the law of the earth: eat or be eaten. The strong devoured the weak the world over. And the so-called civilized man, as the simple Hillman, advertised his station in life by the number of heads he had lopped off.

Drozak was coming home empty-handed. He brought no riches, no trophies, to lay at his father's feet to enhance that veteran Hillman's station among his people. The glitter and bauble of the outside world, Drozak had thought, would corrupt, not enhance, his father. But since he had reached the jungle there had been signs—favorable signs. First there was the male peacock with the three crowns the color of the sun at dawn, then the lemur that had three nights in a row haunted him in his dreams with three fiery eyes, and there was the moon he had traveled under with three bright rings around it.

Drozak lay down on the cool ferns of the floor of the savannah, turned his face directly to the straight down stream of yellow and gold sun rays and fell to dreaming of his tiny village, hidden in a warm and fertile valley at the foot of towering Kinchinjunga, a vast distance away. He thought of his father's hut, and he saw again the neat rows of smoked and dried heads with their black hair streaming unusually long from their shrunken but perfectly preserved faces. Like the gleaming automobiles of the missionary's world or the shiny medallions on the shoulders of men of war, these trophies denoted his father's rank amongst the Hillmen. And he remembered the fine feasts, with all the village attending, that had followed the gaining of each trophy. He wondered if his father had added to his fine collection, improved his standing during his son's absence. The he envisioned that venerable native, a tall, lean but powerful Hillman with hollow cheeks and the same sunken, expressionless eyes as himself. It was then that he heard the plane.

Drozak opened his eyes. A gleaming huge bird of stiff wings skimmed over the jungle treetops, coughing and spitting like a sick monster and rumbling intermittently in its mighty throat. It came across the abandoned field, circled, and then began a long glide downward. Drozak's heart quickened when he saw that its tail was a structure of three shining fins. He stepped back into the jungle wall.

The plane's wheels, upon touching the deceptively firm-looking green, immediately imbedded hopelessly, and the giant bird went up on its nose, cartwheeled, and came to rest on a crumpled wing. Drozak saw three men emerge from the belly of the demolished plane, now crackling with fire. Two of the men were army officers; their uniforms and trappings told him that they belonged to the United States forces. But the other was different, so different that Drozak's still eyes became deep and intense. He was a tall, fair-skinned man, and his thick light hair of web-like softness and tenuity shone like smooth silk under the horizontal sun rays. He had been injured in the crash and limped badly as he drew himself away from the burning plane. Drozak's attention was focused on the man and he noticed three things: he seemed haughtily amused at the situation; his eyes never left the briefcase which was chained and locked to the wrist of one of the officers; and he was handcuffed.

"The others!" yelled one of the officers, and the two uniforms plunged back into the plane.

In a few seconds they reappeared, dragging after them another officer, unconscious. They laid him in the grass at a safe distance from the plane and, holding their arms up against the flames, crept back toward the plane, shouting something about the pilots. The handcuffed man, seizing his opportunity, limped to the unconscious officer, knelt, came up with an Army .45 and, holding it with both hands, in rapid succession fired two shots into the backs of the men fighting their way to the burning plane. With some difficulty he extracted the key to the handcuffs from a pocket of the unconscious officer and undid the handcuffs. He went forward, shot away the lock securing the briefcase to the wrist of one of the dead men, then dragged himself out of danger.

From the shadows of the ferns and ivy Drozak watched the tall man rip open the flap of the briefcase, dump its contents on the ground, quickly check the thick packs of greenbacks and carefully replace them. He strapped the briefcase securely on his back, ventured near the flaming plane to search the body of the officer from whom he had taken the gun, came away with compass, ammunition belt and other items. He surveyed his surroundings, his eyes sweeping the wall of the forest as the towering flames played against the sunlight in his brilliant hair and shone fierce against his light blue eyes. Drozak remained commingled with the tangled mass of vegetation, blended in the trellised shadows of the forest. He was still as the kallege pheasant, clad in red-browns and russets, that sat her nest underneath the shelter of a jutting boulder; he was silent as the langur monkey that swung his long grey form deftly from a deodar branch overhead. But his sunken eyes keenly followed the man's every move. He saw him consult his compass, then set out, limping across the clearing, and disappear into the jungle. Drozak, keeping to the timberline, skirted the field and picked up his spoor. At a safe distance he followed on padded feet. The two men moved, stopped, moved again, maintaining the fixed distance as if they were puppets fastened to a moving belt.

For five days and nights the Hillman thus stalked the man, who progressed in a sort of grotesque forced march, favoring more and more his lame leg. He shot fowl and game with a deadly accuracy, but ate only what the native considered the inedible parts, unwittingly leaving the delicacies for his stalker. He continually consulted his compass and swore mightily. Finally, unable to force his wounded body further, and hopelessly lost, he dropped from exhaustion. Drozak, from the screen of a thicket saw the man struggle to his feet, stagger a few paces, reel and again crash to the ground. He heard him cry out in a despairing voice: *"Mein Gott im Himmel!"* He did not rise again.

Under the lean-to, which days before he had thatched, Drozak squatted beside the man. With a large, stiff leaf he fanned inquisitive flies away from the invalid. Outside, the long golden shafts of sunlight reached far in through the jungle turning the moss to golden lacery and the ferns to yellow-green filigree. The trees were draped with long streaming tassels of green and brown, which softened every outline. Maidenhair fern trembled on the slopes for a backdrop. Birds who were motley and birds done in sharp, brilliant hues complained in sad half-tones, or serenaded in happy crescendo. The soft air was sweet with the perfume of magnolia blossoms and woodbine. But the Hillman cared nought for this wondrous clime: his attention was wholly on the prostrate white man.

During spells of delirium the man had revealed much about himself. In desultory babble he had spoken of Berlin, Vienna, Prague, Paris, Belgrade, Rome. He shouted orders in German. He cursed the Allies, Nürnberg justice, policemen. He whined about jail; he boasted about escape, murder and robbery, flight. He cringed and whimpered and cowered. Once in a wild spasm of fearful delirium he sat up, desperately clutching the briefcase stuffed full of money. "It's mine!" he screamed. "It belongs to me. *SS-Obergruppenführer* Müller. A dozen men I've killed for it! I'll kill a hundred! You can't take me back to prison. I'll not rot away my life in a stinking cell. You can't take away my fortune, my stone wall between me and the world of fools. *Ich bin SS-Obergruppenführer, ein Über-mensch*, understand!* What I take by force is mine!"

On a still afternoon Müller's eyes fluttered, slowly opened. Drozak watched him placidly. He tried his leg, smiled faintly when it moved without pain. Sitting up, he saw it was encased in a plaster of leaves and a substance which resembled an admixture of mud and tar. Examining it wonderingly, he muttered, *"Verdammt noch mal!"*

"You get big sleep."

Müller jerked his head sideways and stared with wide, fearful eyes at the implacable Hillman, who sat on his haunches behind and above him. Quickly he cast around for his pistol, his knife. They were gone. He trembled with fear.

"Your leg, very bad leg. I fix."

Müller slowly regained himself, pondered for a long time, reached out cautiously and drew the briefcase to him.

"Look here, boy," he said to the expressionless Drozak, "I do not know why you do this for me. I will give you money. You understand money?" He patted the fat briefcase.

"Drozak understand."

"Good! You get me safely out of this jungle—any place where I can get a train, a boat, an airplane—and I will give you much money. So much." He indicated several inches with his thumb and forefinger, then eyed the Hillman for reaction. There was none, except:

"O. K. You follow me."

They set out, slowly at first, resting every few minutes, giving Müller's leg back its strength gradually. Drozak struck the trail, always confident of his way. Müller's compass had disappeared along with his weapons, so he was forced to place his entire trust in the little uncommunicative Hillman, while clinging hopefully to his fat briefcase. Drozak foraged for

---

* *Obergruppenführer* was the equivalent rank in the SS to Colonel. *Übermensch* means Superman. Was much played up by the Nazis.

herbs, berries, fruit and certain fat lizards and full-bodied insects. The white man ate the fruit, herbs and berries but disdained the others. For him Drozak occasionally caught a young pheasant or skinned a small furred animal. They made good progress. Until they descended into a murky, stifling valley.

The heat speared down and seared and steamed the dank jungle valley. Trees became denser, and from their bases to their topmost twigs they were covered with a thick coat of brown and green. And whenever the ferns failed, crept the ivy, winding its dull green trail over fallen trunks or seeking to hide every stump of half-dead tree. The vapor was thick and lay heaped unevenly about the treetrunks, flowers the size of cabbages, and bushes; or it drifted in coils over the creepers, clinging close to the jungle floor trying to conceal from view the scorpions, lizards and other crawling ceatures of low life. Great shining drops of moisture fell from the moss stalactite, glistened for a moment as they passed through rays of light, and steamed almost instantly as they struck the hot sponge-like carpet of the glade. Winged and stinged insects invaded the air by countless thousands. And through the sticky nights the Hillman sat in the darkness fanning at great mosquitoes that feasted from the white man's soft, luscious, sweet skin.

Drozak quickened the pace, for well he knew that the white man must reach the highlands soon or be struck down by fever. But Müller weakened and grumbled, and the going became tedious. Finally Müller went down. So thoroughly was he saturated and so completely did he give up, that he seemed to strike the verdure mat with every part of his body at once. They were at the bottom of the valley. In the far distance Drozak could see the icy slopes, and from the peaks there came a slight, indistinct murmur of chill breeze. But in this steaming hell he knew the white man would quickly die. He knelt beside Müller, lifted him up, and with the limp white man jackknifed across his shoulder, lugged him onward toward the cool hills—and life.

There were times when they made fair progress: when Drozak urged the semi-conscious Müller forward under his own power. And there were times when they made no progress at all: when the white man lay on the slopes, his lips moving sluggishly, without words, while his mind roamed the haunts and dens of the great capitals. The Hillman saw his charge slowly slipping over the edge of the world. His face was a leaden hue, and the emaciation was so extreme that the skin was broken through by cheek bones. His eye-lids, when not flung wide, displaying a glassy roll of sickly blue, were drawn nearly closed so as to reveal only a white line of the ball. Tenderly Drozak bathed his face in snow-water, which trickled down from the ice caps; and he pried open his parched lips and forced the juice of wild fruits between them.

By dint of superhuman effort and heart of oak, the Hillman labored Müller forward until they reached a land of deodars and silver firs, whose mighty columns rose straight from their bed of fallen needles. The foliage was sparse and the land silent. But the air was cool and sweet. No singing birds, no chippering and busy monkeys, no laughing peacocks. A shuffle among the fir shrubs indicated a half-grown bear pushing through the underbrush. Ever upward, toward strength and health, the Hillman pushed his man.

When Drozak propelled Müller, now a mere rattle of bones, over the ridge the forest was a dazzling white. A soft carpet of snow covered all the primroses and anemones, and Christmassed the pines and spruces. Then the little Hillman's heart rejoiced, for he saw Müller's head become amazingly clear and his body generate strength. They descended, in clear sunshine, into a tropical valley where the air was redolent with eternal blossoms. Drozak deposited Müller beside a softly tinkling, lapis lazuli stream and quickly constructed a hut of grass, leaves, branches, mud and whatever came to hand. He went away and returned with therapeutic but palatable herbs, great melons, enormous bananas, delectable oranges and other strange sweet fruits; and lo!—a suckling pig, which he roasted over a slow fire.

They feasted and fattened in the most wonderful climate in the world, mild and pleasant, and with the loveliest scenery. To the east of them towered the unbelievably high and glorious Kinchinjunga itself, a crystal of palest tint resting lightly in the clear-cut sapphire sky with the overpowering expression of stability. Small thankful atoms were these two—the little brown man with the still sunken eyes—and the tall white man —moving in the folds of the earth; and in an immediate world that was lovely, beautifully draped with blossoming vines, musical with the cooing of spotted doves. Each smiled inwardly with a purpose as far removed from the other as the very poles of the earth. The white man had his fat bag of money, his stone wall between him and the world that sought—and rightly so if the laws of man are to be respected—to destroy him. Drozak's secret heart was his own.

"Look here, my little man," Müller said, dreaming now of soft white shoulders, full red lips and lascivious glances from underneath long jetty lashes, and of the glittering lights of great cities, "How much further?"

"We go over yon hill. Maybe one—two hour."

"What!" Müller exclaimed. "That close to transportation back to civilized country! Hurry! Hurry, little man!" His heart sang. He patted his stuffed briefcase and lengthened his stride.

Drozak led him down *yon* hill not to a boat or an airplane or a train, but to a native village of low, long thatched bungalows. "We visit my father."

"I've no time for visits with a stupid native! Where's the boat? How do I get out of here?"

Grumbling and cursing the Hillman, Müller followed, stubbornly demanding transportation "out of this damned hole!"

The little Hillman found that his father still wore the bone sharpened at both ends thrust through one flange of his nose. He spoke rapidly with him in their native tongue, and with a wave of his arm indicated the white man. The father turned his stolid, sunken eyes on Müller, surveyed him from foot to head, and his gaze rested a long time on the round, fat arms and white chest, which were bare. Then he admired the golden billows of thick and light, supple and brilliant hair that looked like new honey under a bright sun. He then stepped forward and placed a hand on his son's shoulder. And for the first time the little Hillman's eyes gave a sign—a momentary gleam only.

Müller's cheeks drained. "Come! The boat. There must be a river out of here." His voice was leaded, anxious. "Money. Remember? You get much money. You be rich—see!" He tore open his briefcase and flung two bales of greenbacks at Drozak's feet.

The father turned and disappeared into the hut. When Drozak made no effort to reach for the money, only looked placidly up into the white man's face, Müller seized him by the shoulder. "Get me out of here!" he growled.

Müller was about to kick the little Hillman when he saw the father reappear with that for which he had gone inside—an excessively long and heavy knife. Müller faltered back. The briefcase slipped from his trembling hands, it contents spilling.

Drozak glanced at the scattered packs of money, stepped forward and kicked them out of the way, toward a trash heap nearby. He swung his gaze above his father's door. There were two new heads; they were the same as the others, black-skinned and with black hair. He turned his eyes on Müller and saw the answer to the cycle of *three's* which had hounded him. Here was the third head—and what a head! With this brilliant prize his father's station in the village would soar and his importance would become reknown throughout the jungle. He glanced back toward the rows of thatched huts. In front of each was now gathered a small group of natives—father, mother and a child or two. All were looking with intent gaze and drooping lips at the fair and fat and healthy Müller.

"My father, he gets very pretty trophy," Drozak said to the realizing Müller. "And Drozak will give fine feast for everybody."

A sob lengthening into a whimper escaped from Müller. And the still eyes of the little Hillman saw in his face the fierce bitterness with which the white man regretted, for the first time in his life, the pure strain in himself which made his hair so blond and brilliant.

LILO

This is the story of what happened to Lilo Markgraf and her sister Marlene after the Americans entered Hitler's fallen Reich capital. It might be called a short sequel to "T h e B i g R a p e." I have been flooded with requests to write such a story. And I have been asked many questions about Lilo . . . Yes, I knew a Lilo. The name is fictitious but the girl is factual, and the blonde place in her hair was real. I have watched her fascinating one-sided smile hours on end, while I listened to her resolute voice as she related her experiences under the Russian rape of Berlin. I have seen her large slate-blue eyes ablaze with hatred for the invaders (she considered all the allies "invaders"). I have seen them melt with compassion for the defeated Germans. I have seen them, on other occasions, shine with all the bright passions of the ardent woman she was. I have seen her in happy, carefree moods, with the scars of the war put temporarily behind her. I have waited for her in the hallway of her house on Goethe Strasse, as she came down the stairs smiling and posing for me in all the glory of her feminine graces, and wearing her one and only evening gown, which was form-fitting and revealing and the color of a field of mustard under a blazing moon. I have seen her take off that gown.

James Wakefield Burke

It was, as I have said, at the American Press Center in Berlin that I first saw Lilo. The time was shortly after the former Reich capital had fallen to the Red Army and the

148

Russians had raped the city, sparing not even the very young nor the hideously aged. The Allies had been admitted to the city and order restored. Lilo came to the Press Center looking for a job. Lieutenant Woodson put her on the teletype machines and she turned out to be a very good operator.

Lilo Markgraf was a tall girl, with large, wide-set eyes and a nice figure. The blonde streak in her hair intrigued me and I was later to verify that it was genuine. Her resolute eyes were a deep blue and made an astounding humanity out of a strong face which would otherwise perhaps have seemed somewhat severe. Her nose was large and straight and when she smiled her mobile mouth went up in a one-sided, crooked smile. It was not a derisive smile but a friendly, captivating one. She was attractive and sensuous, yet there was something interdictive about the girl. She seemed remote yet warm: loving and cruel, lonely and friendly, wild and domestic. The first time I saw her she reminded me (as she did on many occasions afterward) of a kitten on the threshold, undecided whether to turn round and run away or to come in. You were not sure that you wanted her to come in. But if she should, you felt you would like to stroke her gently, feel her under your hand, hear her purr. You could swear you were meant to blend—or collide—with her. But you had to take a chance. There seemed to be a fate, a fulfillment, a perfection of logic about it. She was for the bold and the challenging.

Her father's house on Goethe Strasse was requisitioned for a press billet and I took the master bedroom, at the head of the stairway. Lilo and her sister, Marlene, were living in a small room on the third floor, across from the one occupied by her mother and father. These had once been the servants' quarters. Lilo's mother was serving as housekeeper, by direction of the Occupation Forces. There were half a dozen other correspondents living in the house, but for the most part they came and went—transients. Sam Green and I were more or less permanent. Sam Green was with a Chicago newspaper which was known to be broadly liberal. Sam himself was an extreme leftist, which was at that time considered fashionable, if not commendable. He carried a deep resentment against all Germans, called them all Nazis, and believed them to be collectively guilty. Naturally, on first sight he did not like Lilo. But Sam and Marlene struck a common accord through their mutual hatred for the Nazis. In the last days of the fighting, Marlene's fiance, Major Paul Hartmann, had been murdered by a fanatic SS sergeant who rejected Hartmann's order to give up the defense of a doomed bunker.

Marlene had long shapely legs, like Lilo's, and her hips were attractive and sensuous in motion. Her skin was smooth and white, her mouth full and red, and her aureate hair shone brightly like gold mark pieces in the sun. Her eyes were a light blue that sometimes changed to a curious green, and occasionally they shone with a dreamy, unaware negligence. But when she was excited or angry they could dance with laughter or shine with hard brilliance. The presence of Marlene made you glad: glad that you were there and that you were looking at her.

Occasionally Sam Green and I took Lilo and Marlene to dinner at the Press Club. In those days fraternization was forbidden by an army directive, but the members of the Press Club ignored the regulation. On more than one occasion I have seen Generals Eisenhower, McNarney, Clay and other high brass present when the place was filled to overflowing with Fräuleins. Also, at this time, it was not uncommon to see high-ranking Russians among the guests.

One night we were sitting at the gas fireplace talking with some correspondents. Sam was at the bar drinking with friends. It was a big Saturday night party. General Clay had dropped in for a few minutes. But Colonel Howley, the Berlin Commandant, stayed until dawn. Sam came over, his arms flung around a Russian major's shoulders. He was pretty drunk. "Come here, Marlene," he called. "I want you to meet a pal of mine."

Marlene started to get up but when she saw the Russian she froze, just sat there, half-turned in her chair, staring coldly at him.

"Alex wants to dance with you, Marlene. Don't you, Alex? Alex, this is one of the Fräuleins you may have missed when you took Berlin." Sam gave a raucous laugh. "Marlene, this is my pal, Alex."

The Red Army officer bowed, smiled and stepped forward, extending his hand to Marlene. The girl continued to fix him with cold bitter eyes. He looked foolish, standing with back bent and hand extended. Sam staggered forward. "Get on your feet and dance with Alex!" he ordered.

"I don't care to dance," she replied.

"So! . . ." Sam took her by the shoulders as if to pull her to her feet. "You insult an Ally, you—you damn Fräulein!"

Jack Crane, sitting next to me, was on his feet. "Leave her alone, Sam. If she doesn't want to dance, well then she doesn't."

"Goddamn you, Crane, keep out of this. She's a guest in our club and she's insulted a member of the Occupation Forces."

"Leave her alone!" It was Lilo. She stepped between Sam and Marlene, her eyes flashing.

"Come on, forget it. I'll buy you a drink." I led him over to the bar while he grumbled about the "damn arrogant krauts" and "that Goddamn reactionary, Crane."

Early in November I came down with dysentery, which was raging in Berlin. It was easy to get into the army hospital but hard to get out: you just walked in but a series of diagnoses and a batch of paperwork was required to discharge you. So I elected to stay in my billet and diet and let the malady run its uncomfortable course. Lilo looked after me. She dropped in several times every day, ran my errands, and in the evenings we talked. She told me much about the fall of Berlin, related in detail how Marlene and her mother had been raped by two Red Army soldiers. I understood Marlene's violent attitude against dancing with the Russian major. I asked Lilo if she had been raped. She looked me straight in the eyes and said "No."

During my illness an incident occurred which gave rise to a rumor that almost convinced me that she spoke the truth. One evening, instead of sitting with me, she went to visit some friends of the family down in the Kurfürstendamm district. She did not come home that night. Next day she explained that she had forgotten to take her key with her, and when she got home she couldn't get in. She had pounded on both front and back doors but couldn't raise anybody. So she went next door to the Stars and Stripes house.

"You stayed there?" I asked, somewhat surprised.

"Yes. Duke Maling took me in," she said quite calmly.

I didn't ask any more questions. *I* was embarrassed.

In the next days the whole story came out; Duke Maling was a loquacious fellow. It was a cold night with a wet snow blowing and the wind was raw and pointed. Obviously she couldn't stay outside all night without freezing, she rang the Stars and Stripes bell. Duke let her in. She asked him simply if she could stay there for the night. Thinking himself in luck, Duke cheerfully invited her into his room, opened a bottle of bourbon. Oh, he made a proper effort that night, he told around the Press Club, but the girl resisted him. Next morning he tried his hand once more, he said, and he made a startling discovery. "Imagine!" he snickered. "She was a virgin! And me, old 'sure lay' Maling, finding her on my doorstep on a cold, cold night! You fellows know me. I wouldn't touch a *virgin*."

Of course nobody believed that last part of Maling's story. But everyone did accept the fact that Lilo was a virgin; and they believed that she valiantly fought him off in order to

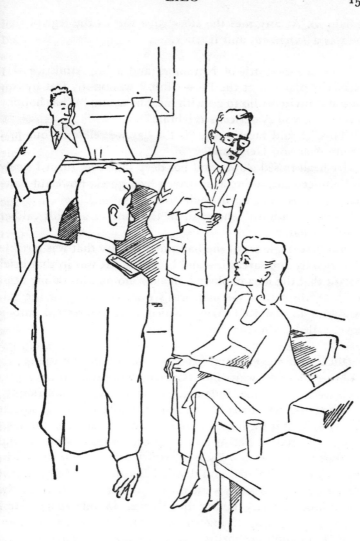

remain so. At any rate the story gave rise to the legend that she was a *Jungfrau,* and it stuck.

Came the eleventh of November and a big Armistice Day party was planned at the Press Club. I was on my feet by this time and invited Lilo to go with me. She asked, "What holiday is this that you Americans celebrate?"

"This," I said facetiously, "is the day we celebrate our *first* victory over you Germans."

Her head raised slowly and her deep blue eyes turned steely and plunged into mine as if driven by a quick, powerful hammer. Her lips went up in their crooked smile.

"Congratulations!" she said, in the tone of a small caliber pistol discharged.

Into that single word she had put a quality that was terrible and friendly and sarcastic—and humorous. It was in that brief instant that the idea exploded, in slow motion, inside my head to write, through a German girl's eyes, the story of the fall of Berlin to the Red Army, which later burgeoned into a novel called "The Big Rape."

During the next several years, we in Berlin saw the generating of the cold war. The Russians withdrew entirely into their sector, became independent and actively unfriendly. Their course was to split the world, while the West sought vainly to hold it together by patience, diplomacy, compromise. But the Soviets in Berlin had their orders from Moscow, and so came the Berlin Blockade of 1948-49. The world turned its uneasy eyes on isolated and divided Berlin and trembled. But we inside the blockade went on about our little lives in the dark, brooding city taking the danger in our stride. Herr Markgraf was busy trying to resurrect his milling business. The Occupation authorities were helping him; anybody who could produce bread was an asset to our side. Already he was operating his bakery in Spandau on a limited scale. There were long evenings by candlelight with nothing to do. Lilo and I talked: little by little her story came out: I made mental notes, later jotted them down.

About this time Marlene had a piece of luck. She met a very substantial American who fell in love with her. Lieutenant Colonel Thomas Means, Counter Intelligence Corps, was a pleasant fellow about thirty-three or -four years of age. He was a tall and muscular man with dark hair, a friendly face and a blunt nose which refined upward to where it joined a pair of strong and honest eyebrows. A career officer, he had a good record and came from a family of honored name. He and Marlene became engaged and he assumed an informal position in the family circle.

The blockade ended with a victory for the Germans. I say a victory for the Germans, for the world remained more rigidly divided than ever, and it was obvious that whichever side possessed Germany would eventually control Europe. So the Americans adopted a new policy intended to win the West German people by indulgence and coddling. As fast as the Allies could decently do so they shed occupation controls and sought to thrust on the Germans state autonomy. Marshall money was poured in almost as if squirted from a firehose, and Nazis great and small were turned out of jail and put to work cheek by jowl with good Germans who had been painstakingly "de-Nazified." Indeed, regret was expressed in certain quarters that we had irresponsibly hanged some very excellent Nazis. The currency reform brought about by money printed in Washington and backed up by United States dollars was working wonders. And we were telling the world that the Germans were a bunch of splendid fellows—really: they were a hardworking, industrious, frugal, honest people who had an incomparable sense for organization. Yes, we had to have these fellows on our side.

My news agency sent me on a prolonged junket to Italy, Africa, Turkey and the Near East. When I got back to Berlin I asked for my old room in the Markgraf house and was told it was occupied, but was given another one across the hall from it. Lilo was still working for the Press Center but Lieutenant Woodson had been rotated, and there were new faces all over the place. Many of the old-time hard-bitten war correspondents were gone. Bright, eager youngsters, sent out from their home offices to get a taste of foreign work, and middleaged faded women staff writers, no doubt ex-mistresses of publishers and managing editors despatched abroad to make way for younger and fresher talent, were cluttering up the place.

Sam Green was gone, too. It had been a long time. The Americans were no longer conducting themselves like conquerors, but rather as self-conscious interlopers. And the Germans were making the most of it. They were becoming haughty and arrogant: no more scraping and bowing at the feet of the Allies. The *Übermensch* attitude that Sam Green used to complain about was amazingly manifest. When correspondents discussed the German people they often quoted, perhaps harshly and too unkindly, the long-departed war correspondent, Sam Green. They remembered such statements of Sam's as: "There are a lot of good Germans—out in the cemeteries!" and "These krauts are insufferable: they're either at your feet or at your throat!" and "The best Germans are clubbed Germans! Club 'em as often as they shake your hand: before breakfast, after breakfast: before lunch, after lunch: before dinner, after dinner: before going to bed. And if the bastards dream at night, club 'em in their sleep!" Well, Sam was gone, his newspaper had folded; notwithstanding, the seeds Sam Green had sown were now great poison oaks.

I was curious to know who was living in my old room and when I checked in at the Markgraf house I went and knocked at the door. Marlene opened it. She had been living there for some time, she told me. I wondered how she had managed it. That night when I took Lilo to dinner I got a fill-in on many things. She told me that Colonel Means had gotten the master bedroom assigned to Marlene. A tacit arrangement had been reached between the Colonel, Marlene, Papa and Mama whereby Marlene slept with the Colonel in his quarters one night, and the next he spent with her at the Markgraf house. Lilo told me this without the slightest prudishness, as if it were quite customary; maybe so, but I had never heard of this practice in Tennessee, where I came from. I dropped the subject.

We retired to a cozy corner and talked until early in the morning. Papa had gotten Marshall aid and his business was rapidly expanding and becoming quite prosperous. They hoped to get the house derequisitioned shortly. Colonel Means was doing what he could to expedite the matter. Lilo talked a great deal about politics. Whenever she mentioned the new German army her face brightened and her eyes shone with pride, and I was reminded of another statement Sam Green had made: "Nationalism is patriotism with a superiority complex." And I began to suspect that the Germans, given power, would take another fling at world aggression, as Sam had often predicted. "Any alliance between the Germans and any European, as well as Asian, is possible," he used to say.

During the months that followed I devoted all my spare time to my manuscript, seeing and talking with Lilo as frequently as possible. She was free most of the time, for the erroneous notion that she was a virgin had become accepted as a hard, if unfortunate, fact and the correspondents ceased to bother her. I was glad, for this left her free to give me more information, which went into my book. Some of the newcomers sprang at the chance to date her, either distrusting the legend or through a sense of personal conceit and vanity, but dropped her after one or two dates. There were plenty of girls at hand with whom they could sleep without preliminaries. These erudite youngsters dubbed her *"Die schöne Jungfrau."*

One night Jack Crane, Lilo and I were talking about the new German army. (Now that I think back on it, I distinctly recall that it was Lilo who brought this subject up; it was her favorite topic.) Crane was against it altogether.

"Let's arm these people, make them a buffer between the East and West," I said. "Then we can get out. I don't like the role of 'occupier.' "

"How do you know which way they'll shoot?" Crane asked quietly.

"They've got to be on our side!" I retorted. "Look what we've done for them."

Crane, a brilliant and profound writer, said coolly, "It is a psychological fact that the more you help a person the less he likes you and the more you like him. If you continue to help him he may even come to bear a genuine hatred for you. We've about reached that point with the Germans. They bear a deep resentment, if not actual hatred, for us."

"We don't want to fight for anybody," Lilo said. "If we ever fight again, we will fight only for ourselves, under our own leaders—and only when we are sure of victory." Her eyes shone with a dream of future glory. "Next time we'll give a better account of ourselves. Under Hitler's leadership we had only imaginary grievances against our neighbors. But now we have real grievances, and therefore we must be harder than ever before. When we lost this war, rightful territories were taken away from us. One day we will get them back. Every German knows this and keeps it clearly in mind. It is a silent but dedicated duty with him. That is why we will never admit to ourselves that we were beaten in Hitler's war. Certainly we lost it; but we were not beaten." She hesitated a moment, while her face became clouded with a mixture of hate and sorrow. "And we have suffered much because we lost it."

Crane leaned over, put his finger hard between her breasts. "Let me correct that last statement, Lilo. You Germans have suffered not because you lost the war, but because you *started* it."

Her eyes flashed, then she caught herself. Her one-sided smile came to her face. She brushed his finger away. "Sorry," she said.

One night along about seven o'clock when I came home and started up the stairs to my room, I met Lilo coming down the stairway with a strange man. He was a tall, fair-skinned civilian, and I noticed particularly his eyes, because they were of such a cold, steely hue. He looked quickly at me, took Lilo by the arm and brushed past me and out the door with her. She did not speak, and gave no sign whatsoever. I was puzzled but thought not much of it. Strange things happened in Berlin.

Next day however, when I did not find her on the job at the Press Center I went back to the house and knocked on Marlene's door. Nobody was there. Back at the Press Center I asked the officer in charge why Lilo wasn't working. He supposed she was sick; no, she hadn't notified anybody of her absence. I telephoned Colonel Means' office and a secretary told me he was in the Zone, had been for several days. I dismissed the matter from my mind, but that night found myself sitting in my room trying to read and listening for one of the girls to come up the stairs.

About eleven o'clock I heard their voices. I met them on the landing. Lilo tried to smile casually, but I saw the strain in her face. "What happened?" I asked.

"Nothing, why?" She opened the door to Marlene's room and Marlene went in without speaking to me. I noticed that she was in no mood to face anybody.

"I saw you leaving last night with a mysterious man. The

Press Center couldn't account for you today. If there's anything I can do . . ."

"Nothing," she hastened to reply. "Nothing is wrong, really. I'll see you tomorrow. Please, we're very tired . . ."

She went into Marlene's room and I presume immediately to bed, for neither of them came out that night.

It is likely that I never would have found out what happened but for the dead man on the back lawn.

The man I had seen coming down the stairs with Lilo, it finally came out, was MVD agent, Pavel Ivanov, of the Russian Secret Police. Pavel Ivanov had been an NKVD captain in the early days of the occupation of Berlin, and he and Lilo had had more than a casual acquaintance. They had lived together, briefly, in the master bedroom of the Markgraf house which was now used by Marlene and Colonel Means. Lilo had deliberately yielded to the Russian officer as the lesser of two evils: by becoming Ivanov's mistress she had saved herself from the rape and brutality of the Red Army soldiers.

A few minutes before I had seen her leaving with him, as the story unfolded, Lilo had just come in from the Press Center. Hardly was she in her room when there came a guarded rap on the door. She opened it, and Pavel slipped in, locked the door behind him. Lilo's hand went to her mouth, stifling a little gasp.

"Do I surprise you, Liselotte?" he said in flawless German. (He had always preferred to call her Liselotte, spurning the contracted Lilo.)

She faced him, speechless. Of a sudden she became alarmed. She knew now that Marlene's absence from the house all day was of a serious nature. There were a thousand things she could have said to Pavel Ivanov. But she uttered only one statement: "You have Marlene."

"That's why I'm here." He held up a reassuring hand. "She's all right. No harm has come to her—yet. I am here to tell you that you must come with me, too. I have given instructions if I am not back within an hour to place your sister under another's jurisdiction. Then I can no longer promise she will be safe. You will come, of course."

Lilo stood looking at this man whom she had known long ago, in whose arms she had once found protection and care, and with whom she had been able to completely release herself in rare moments of intimacy. She tried to find the kindliness, the smiling boyish joy that used to light up that face at the sight of her. She was looking into the face of an older—a much older-looking—Pavel Ivanov: a face that belonged not to a man but to a regime, an organization, a machine: a face

that could not leave the burden of duty at the office and come at night to the tender arms of a woman. The Pavel she knew long ago could manage this; but not this man. There was a cold awareness about the eyes. They seemed now to be narrow-set and the tiny lines that fanned outward from them were the fruits of uneasiness and constant watchfulness; the hard cast of the face bespoke suspicion. Yet he was not a complete stranger. She had long ago been permitted glimpses of him. There had been times when she could see this man trying to outgrow and overcome the youngish Captain Pavel Ivanov in whose arms she used to lie with such infinite rapture. That promising young man was, obviously, defunct and this man had risen up in his stead. He was holding Marlene somewhere in the Russian sector of the city. She knew what she had to do, and she did not hesitate. "I'll come with you," she said.

In Karlshorst, in the Russian sector of the city, the black sedan pulled up to a grey stone building and Pavel Ivanov ushered her into a large room comfortably appointed with Oriental rugs and expensive furniture. Save for the desk in one corner it might have been the drawing room of a rich post-war West German industrialist. "May I see my sister now?" she asked.

"First I want to explain why you are both here."

"Where is she?"

"She's here. In this building. You'll see her soon. Do you want to hear what it is all about first?"

"Please explain—if you can."

"Your sister is engaged to a Lieutenant Colonel Thomas A. Means, of the United States Army Counter Intelligence Corps . . ."

Lilo gave a little mocking laugh, breaking in on him. "You want to turn her into a spy for the Russians. Pavel, you disappoint me." She smiled her crooked smile. "Yes, you disappoint me, Pavel."

The man's face hardened; he continued. "We want only one piece of information, which we believe she can get for us. Just a name, nothing more. There is a traitor to the Motherland on the staff of our embassy on Unter den Linden. Important information is being relayed to Counter Intelligence agents. We don't know who the traitor is. We want his name. Your Colonel Means can give it to us."

"She'd die before she'd help a Russian. Have you forgotten what happened to her and Mama at Volkholz?"

"She's a defiant one, all right. We found that out during the interrogation. Too bad she cannot forget that little unfortunate incident with those two soldiers. That was a long time ago."

" 'Little unfortunate incident!' How little you Russians will ever understand German women!"

"That's why you are here. You're the sensible one. You must convince her that she must co-operate with us in this matter."

"Or . . . ?"

He took her by the shoulders, gently, his eyes softening. "Liselotte, I have not forgotten you. You have been in my mind ever since that day we said *Auf Wiedersehen* on Goethe Strasse years ago. I do not want any harm to come to you or your sister. I have staked my career on this mission. I have assured my superiors that I will deliver the name of the traitor to them. I have taken full responsibility in this matter. I cannot fail. It would mean my finish. If you cannot make Marlene see what she has to do, then I will be forced to use drastic measures."

"You would kill us?"

"Rather than fail in my duty—yes. But we have many other methods before that becomes necessary. Some very effective ones. For instance, if you should simply disappear until your sister consents to bring us the name of the man we want . . ."

Lilo sat down on a divan, the iron of defiance draining out of her. "Give me a cigarette, Pavel."

Immediately he was chivalrous. He flipped open his cigarette case, whirled the flint-wheel of his lighter. A little smile broke upon his lips.

"Ah, Liselotte! You're being sensible."

"You realize that you're asking my sister to betray the man she will marry, the man with whom she must spend the rest of her life."

"He's an American, *Liebling*. Think what the Americans have done to you, to your country. Whose bombs killed your people and destroyed your homes, your cities? It was American planes and bombs, not Russian, that killed your women and children indiscriminately. We killed German soldiers, yes. And your soldiers killed us. We killed each other bravely, on the field of battle. The Americans killed cowardly, killed those who could not fight back. They came from a distant continent, across an entire ocean to get at you, to kill you. *They* invaded you! And look at your people today. A decade has gone by and you are still their captives. You are helplessly chained to their capitalistic greed."

He sat down beside her, placed an arm around her shoulder. "You cannot hate us, Liselotte. You cannot hate *me*. You must make Marlene see that what she must do for us is not wrong. It is *right*. We are your friends. We are working feverishly night and day planning your deliverance from these imperialistic gangsters."

He lifted her face, kissed her. Slowly, her arm went along his shoulder, around his neck. She drew him close, pressed her breasts hard against him. She returned his kiss; and when his passion mounted, she released him. He clung to her for a long moment and his flushed face, his shining eyes, told her what she wanted to know: that the memory of the young Captain Ivanov in the man still loved her. He let her go, smiled. "Now I will take you to your sister."

The building to which Pavel had brought Lilo was a sub-headquarters for the Secret Police. The upstairs was his apartment. It was a large five-room affair and was policed by three armed plainclothes MVD officers. Marlene was there, and to Lilo's relief was unharmed but in a severe state of anxiety. A grand dinner was prepared and they ate under the surveillance of the guards, who stood erect against the wall beside the three doors to the room. After dinner, liquers and vodka were served. Lilo and Marlene did not partake of the beverages but Pavel drank freely and soon became somewhat loquacious. He tried to recall favorably the "good old days of '45." He spoke about the conquest and occupation of Berlin by the Red soldiers as if they really were good times, completely ignoring the vast amount of suffering and dying they brought to the Berliners.

The vodka shone in Pavel's flushed face, and his eyes became eager and avid.

He had slid his chair over next to Lilo's, and with an arm around her was continually nibbling at her neck and trying to kiss her. Finally Lilo, irritated, said, "Pavel, Marlene and I are very tired. May we go to bed?"

"Fine idea!" he agreed enthusiastically, and shouted an order to the guards in Russian.

Two of them came and escorted the girls from the room and down the hallway. Pavel followed in a rather careless manner, humming a Russian tune. The guards paused before a bedroom, ushered Marlene in, shut and locked the door, then took Lilo to the big room at the end of the hall. Pavel followed her in, closed and bolted the door.

"Are you drunk, Pavel?" she asked, looking at him with cold, level eyes.

"Certainly not," he replied, removing his coat.

"Then listen to me. You should know that you can't force me to sleep with you."

"I know that, *Liebling*. I thought you would do so willingly, since we are going to work together. If not, I'm prepared to persuade you."

"Persuade me?"

"Marlene is safe as long as I do not call out to the guards. Now, if you are a sensible girl . . ."

Lilo went to the window, drew back the curtain and gazed through the iron bars out at the black, deserted street below. She clenched her fists to keep back the trembling rage that was tearing through her body. She was caught, tricked, overpowered—trapped completely. There was nothing in the world she could do about it.

Next morning Lilo lay for a long time with her eyes wide open, looking straight up at the ceiling. Her mind was filled with a desperate resolution. Beside her Pavel Ivanov slept the soothed, relaxed, peaceful sleep of a spent and emptied man. Finally he stirred, and she felt his hand gently caressing her smooth thigh. He opened his eyes and drew her close to him. She recalled out of the past that his passion early in the morning had always surpassed that of the night before. She closed her eyes and tried to think of herself as a helpless willow, bending to the violence of the harsh wind. Sometime afterward, when she spoke, her voice was calm and subdued. "Pavel, you said you only wanted one favor—the name of your traitor."

"That is all."

"Will you trust me?"

"How?"

"Let Marlene and me go back home. Come to me in one week. I promise . . ."

He cut her words with a hard kiss. He was silent for a time. "Do you realize what you're asking, the risk I'd be taking?"

"Yes, Pavel."

He fell silent again. She nuzzled close to him, ran her fingers through the silken hairs on his chest, kissed his ear. "Don't you think I'd want you—like this—again? Don't *you* want me again?" In her voice was the promise of the loot of Paradise.

"Liselotte, I shall want you every single day—like this. I shall always want you . . . I will come to you in one week."

When the girls arrived back home, Lilo had a long talk with her father. Marlene was sent to an aunt in the American Zone where she would be safe. When Colonel Means returned Herr Markgraf explained everything. In a conference with his superiors it was decided that the Colonel's usefulness in Berlin was at an end. He was ordered back to Washington but given a few days leave so that he could marry Marlene. The occupation authorities offered to fly Herr Markgraf and his family out of Berlin but Herr Markgraf refused the offer: his business was flourishing and he would take a chance on remaining. Lilo scoffed at the suggestion of leaving Berlin.

She did not tell her father that she had an assignation with MVD agent Pavel Ivanov.

Pavel came to her at the appointed time. Lilo knew he would come. She knew how deeply stirred he had been by the thought of possessing her again—and again. She had been sure of him. When he appeared she was waiting for him in her room.

"Weren't you afraid to come here?" she said, when he had taken off his coat and proceeded to make himself at home. "I could have laid a trap for you."

"I trust you, *Liebling*. I think I would have come even if I didn't. I've been able to think of nothing but you."

He took her in his arms, trembled with excitement at the contact of her body with his.

"I didn't have to lay a trap for you, Pavel," she said, taking herself out of his arms. "You laid your own trap—and you walked right into it."

"What are you telling me?"

"I haven't got your traitor's name. I never intended getting it. I betrayed you, Pavel. Marlene and Colonel Means are beyond your reach. You can kill me but I don't think you will. It will not get you out of your trap."

The line of his jaw became hard, trembled a little. His face grew pale to the very lips, and there came a blackness about his eyes. He walked slowly up and down in the narrow confines of the room. Finally he spoke, talking as if he were speaking to himself.

"Yes, I shall kill you," he said in a dungeon voice. "I thought that you and I were alike, Liselotte, that I had reached you so completely—physically at least—that you could not fail me. It was the faith I had in myself. For the first time in my life I let my feelings interfere with my official function. Yes, I shall have to kill you. Killing you will be like destroying part of my own body. Therefore I will have punished myself."

"You are right, Pavel. We are alike. I am hard and you are hard. But we are hard for different reasons. You are hard because you are afraid to be otherwise. I am hard because I am a German, and we Germans must be hard to survive. That is how we have become a great people: by being harder than those around us. When you forced me to sleep with you, you became weak but I remained strong. That is how I have beaten you. You are again soft when you talk of killing me. That, I am sure, you have every intention of doing. I cannot stop you. But it will only give you a moment's illusion of hardness. It will not get you out of the trap your softness has sprung on you. Your superiors are bound to liquidate you."

"But first, it is only right that I must kill you. You have betrayed me for the Americans."

"I did not betray you for the Americans. What do I care about them! They are a soft and simple people. They have not learned to be strong by being tough, and therefore I cannot respect them. They are rich and can afford to be soft, an extravagance not meant for us Germans. I can be harder and tougher than all of you, especially when it concerns my sister. When you turned soft at the sight of my body, I could no longer abide you. You gave me the power to betray you, and so I had to do it. If I had not done so I would not have been true to myself."

He struck her a cruel blow in the face. She staggered and fell on the bed. He flung himself on her, and his violence faded away. He buried his head in her hair on her white shoulders and sobbed. His fingers sank into her soft flesh. He kissed her hard again and again, until she could not get her breath. She forced his mouth away from her face, causing his agonized passion to heighten. He tore off her blouse and cupped her white breasts in his trembling hands. He kissed her breasts, her body, her face, her mouth; he kissed her wildly and pathetically. Her voice was in his ear, warm and taunting. "Take me, Pavel. Be soft once more."

He flung himself away from her and staggered to the wall, struggling to get hold of himself. In one continuous movement his hand swept underneath his arm and came out with a revolver. He stepped to the bed and placed its muzzle against her temple. She did not move; she lay calm and still, her round, white breasts rising and falling with her steady breath. Her eyes half opened: their deep blue was like icicle points and they smote him cold. She said softly, "It will not open the trap for you."

The gun was gone from her temple, the door was flung wide. She heard him stumbling down the stairs, heard him going through the dining room, heard the back door open. In a moment the loud, startling explosion of his revolver broke over the back lawn and reverberated over the quiet waters of tiny Waldsee lake. He had escaped from his trap.

GOING DOWN

THE TWO MEN were on the seventy-fifth floor, waiting for the elevator. "Then what happened?" urged the big one with the cigar, evidently a business man.

The younger man was not a business man. He had the keen, steady, searching eyes which come from long hours of vigil or from careful and concentrated attention to an exacting task. His brow was furrowed slightly, and his tanned face had the resolute cast of one accustomed to command and quick decisions. He was a test pilot, and had been relating one of his recent experiences to his cigar-smoking friend. He had become modestly embarrassed and ceased talking when several other persons, also waiting for the elevator, became interested in his story. The big man nudged him. "Go on! You were at seven thousand feet when the plane caught fire . . ."

"Well, I wasn't sure at first that the plane was on fire. Sometimes new engines smoked a little and the fumes were drafted back into the cockpit. Those jobs were far from perfect, many were full of bugs. At that time we didn't know too much about that type of plane. We were working night and day trying to catch up with the enemy's output, and testing was a very risky business at best. When the cockpit got so full of smoke I couldn't see, I slid back the canopy. Then I saw the fire. Tongues of red flame were licking into the cockpit, down by my feet. It was an oil fire. My crankcase was burning."

The elevator dropped into opaque view behind the frosted glass, the doors slid open, the operator called out: "Going down!"

The young man and his friend stepped inside and others crowded in after them. The test pilot continued his story, in his low, modulated voice. ". . . Then I knew it was time to part company with the ship. I had never lost a plane, although there were times, I suppose, when I would have been justified in bailing out. I always tried to bring them in. It was a matter of personal pride with me, I think. Besides, we needed every one of those planes badly at the time. But this one I knew I would have to abandon. It would be only a matter of minutes until the flames reached the fuel tanks, then it would explode. I unsnapped my 'mike,' took off my head-set, stuffed the plane's log book inside my flying jacket, unhooked my safety belt, checked my parachute paraphernalia, pulled the ship's nose high, preparatory to rolling it on its back and spilling myself out. Then I remembered my passenger. . . ."

"Out!—seventieth floor!" The elevator had halted, the operator was holding the doors open. Nobody got out.

The big man with the cigar nudged the pilot. "You had a passenger?"

"Long habit of flying alone had made me completely forget about him. Early that morning Washington had telephoned the plant, requesting the vice president to come at once for an urgent conference. He had commandeered me and the plane to get him there. I recalled the job I had getting him in the gunner's seat and buttoned up. He had never been in one of these planes before. I had handed him up on the wing and pointed to the gunner's compartment, indicating that he should get in. Excited by the prospect of the ride in this fast, new-type plane, he peered helplessly into the narrow confines of the quarters, eyed the metal seat dubiously, turned a bewildered face toward me. 'Okay,' I said, 'I'll help you.'

"Unlatching the machine guns, I swung them out of the way, placed his parachute in the seat and helped him in. Then I snapped on his 'chute harness and adjusted and fastened his safety belt and crash straps. Closing and locking the canopy,

I reset and locked the dual guns overhead. Then I climbed into the pilot's seat in front of him and took off . . ."

"Fiftieth floor!" The elevator operator held the doors open, but nobody got out. The car was now filled and everybody was very quiet, listening to the test pilot's story. "Fiftieth floor—out!" the operator repeated. Nobody stirred. He closed the doors and the elevator cab dropped smoothly down.

"Suddenly I realized that should I jump, my passenger would be doomed, for I had not given him one word of instruction of how to get out in case of an emergency. Pictures flashed through my mind of all the things that could happen as he toiled to extricate himself. I saw him jerking at his canopy, desperately trying to unfasten and telescope it forward, as it normally operates. I knew he would completely ignore the emergency release pin which would instantly jettison the entire top-piece. I had failed to point it out to him. I saw him attempting to release his safety belt and shoulder straps. There was every chance that in his fumbling excitement he would unsnap his 'chute straps instead. He might even pull the rip-cord, filling the compartment with silk. Blown out of the plane, there was every chance that he would become entangled in the plane's empennage and be dragged down with the burning wreck.

"There was no use in my trying to be optimistic. For were my passenger able to open the canopy and squeeze by the locked guns overhead, his chances of making it would still be slim. He didn't know even the first step of abandoning the ship. I had not told him how to avoid the extremely high vertical fin behind him. One little smack from this and he would be knocked unconscious. Then he'd plunge to his death without ever opening his parachute. No, he couldn't possibly make . . ."

"Out—thirtieth floor!" Nobody moved.

"The flames were gaining. But I could still save myself. They say that a doomed man relives his entire life just before the end. I was reliving only a phase of mine, and with a hell of a big regret. I was avidly swearing at myself because I hadn't given my passenger complete directions:—How to jettison the canopy:—How to unlock and swing clear the machine guns overhead:—How to release safety belt and free crash straps:—How to uprise in seat without being blown out and hurled against the vertical fin:—How to slide over the side, head first, and which side to go out, taking advantage of torque:—Why he should go over the side instead of trying to climb out on the wing and jump:—Make sure his hand was on the rip-cord handle before leaving the plane, and how to wait until he was sure he was clear:—Complete instructions on how to contact the ground: land with his back to the wind: run with canopy of 'chute, pulling at the bottom shroud lines to deflate it: in case of landing among trees or in brush, cross legs:—How to free himself from 'chute harness once on ground.

"I looked at my passenger. He was serenely taking in the countryside—and as far as I could tell he didn't have the slightest notion that the ship was on fire. What to do . . ."

"Twentieth floor! Out—twentieth floor. Nobody out? O.K.! Going down!"

"Well, I could have saved myself, all right. But what about my passenger? It would have been easy enough to explain what had happened to him—later. I pictured briefly in my mind what I would tell the board of enquiry. I gave him orders to bail out, abandoned ship myself, and supposed he had done the same. Poor fellow! Too bad he didn't make it.

"But could I do that: He was my responsibility. I couldn't leave him there to die helplessly—alone—in the burning ship. I levelled the plane out. I'd stick with him. Believe me, I wasn't feeling heroic or noble. Actually, I felt like seven kinds of damn fools. I had gotten the poor boob in this predicament —and I just couldn't abandon him . . ."

The elevator stopped and the operator announced: "Main

floor!" The test pilot and his friend stepped out, the latter chewing the stub of his cigar excitedly. They went toward the street. The dozen or so passengers followed in a body. A man shouted, "Hey, hold on a minute, young fellow. What happened after that?"

The pilot was embarrassed. "Sorry, I wasn't aware that you were listening."

"Hell! I belong on the fortieth floor. What happened to your passenger? Go on, young man!"

"Well, I figured I'd try to get the plane down—somehow. By now we were trailing a plume of smoke, and the flames were moving up along the firewall and out toward the wings. Still my passenger didn't know what was going on. He was too busy enjoying the scenery. I knew the route, knew there was a big army air field about fifteen miles on my right. I doubted that I could make it before the fire got to the gas tanks, but it was my best chance. I struck a course for the field, putting my mike and head-set back on and calling for an emergency landing. Instantly the tower came back, clearing the entire area for me. I payed out my altitude grudgingly and held my breath, expecting the ship to blow up at any instant.

"Finally—it seemed ages but actually it was only a matter of seconds—the white, beautiful runways of the field came into view. I cut the engine and made a short steep glide for the nearest strip. On either side of the runway was a fire truck and, not to comfort my agitated nerves, a white ambulance. I was thinking what irony should the plane explode just now. I thought about my young wife, the dinner we had planned for that evening, the friends we would have in, the drinks we would have together. And I thought about the jokes I would make at the expense of the pompous vice president beaming with child-like joy behind me, ignorant that I was carrying his life in my two hands, tenderly, carefully, and walking on tiptoe, ever so softly, and as it were, over the narrow and tottering bridge between Fate and Eternity.

"And I was Goddamn mad at Fate herself. If I was going to be blown to a thousand bits, why in the name of all the little gremlins, did she bring me here to drool at the sight of green fields and solid earth? Had she brought me here, in sight of those glittering, safe runways, merely to drag my nose away as I was about to nibble at the beautiful breast of life? No! she couldn't get away with it! I was mad now, good and sore. I'd tweak the old bag's nose, pinch her nipples. I'd whack her on the bottomside! Goddamn it, I'd make it! I'd put those wheels down on that beckoning runway beneath me. No, I wasn't dying today!

"The plane's wheels touched the concrete, lay to and raced down the strip. I drew the stick back, tailing the ship to the runway, and applied the brakes. The tires squealed, but the heavy aircraft slowed. I flung open my canopy, lifted myself out of the coffin-like seat, kicked the guns from their moorings over my passenger's head, broke open the canopy, began unsnapping his belts. 'Sir!' I shouted. 'Get out of here. We're on fire!'

"And believe me, gentlemen, had I known he could abandon ship with the speed he did, one vice president and one test pilot would have said good-bye to one dive bomber long before. He went out of that narrow hole of a seat like a seed out of a grapefruit. And by the time the asbestos-clad men were swarming over the ship, smothering it with chemical extinguishers, he was halfway to the hangar, running like the very devil, trailing silk from his opened 'chute behind him."

TEST DIVE

YOU ARE FAR UP into the blue, and that detached sensation you get at being miles away from the earth makes you feel like a large smile turned outside in. A smugness overtakes you. Testing the controls, you find that the plane responds obediently and instantly. You test the throttles and find the engine —a full-throated monster—responding readily and earnestly to your slightest touch. You check the instruments and make your entries on the "squawk pad" strapped to your leg. Through the cirrus you fly, upward and upward, playing among those high altitude waifs like a cat with a ball of yarn. You strike your altitude and level off, on the top step. You are ready for the dive.

You check your parachute, see that it is snapped on correctly. You check your safety harness, make sure that the release pin is handy. The canopy emergency release, you determine, is operative and safetied just right.

These things you do, although you know that your engineer and other attendants have checked and rechecked these items before you took off. And you know they are all down there with eyes riveted on the empty, cobalt sky, intently waiting for the first thrilling glimpse of you darting down to the earth. You smile, outwardly now, at the awful doubt you know is raking their souls—doubt about the pull-out. You smile because you know—you don't know how you know, you just know—that everything is going to be all right.

That makes you determined to prove them dead wrong: the designers, the engineers, the mechanics—everyone concerned with the building of the ship. You will do your damnedest to dive it so fast that it will disintegrate. And if it still hangs together after reaching thermal velocity, you swear to tear off its wings in the pull-out. Your mind thus cast, you're ready.

Checking your position, you make the desired compass heading. You take a deep breath *and relax.* Then you shove the stick forward, the nose goes over, and instantly the air-speed indicator needle leaps forward. You plunge the throttles open. The altimeter unwinds like a runaway clock. You don't realize it, but you have violently compressed your lungs full of air and are letting it out in a long, strained grunt.

You look over the nose again, jam the stick full forward, then deliberately trim the elevator control tabs for vertical descent. Whatever scraps, screws and shavings have been left in the monocoque, together with your mask and radio harness float weirdly—suspended in space—before you. There is a mighty and incomprehensible roar in your head which you will never be able to describe.

Now you see the earth racing up at you. But you are not interested in the earth. The airspeed indicator is your lord and master. It has ceased to creep forward; it points wearily and unsteadily at . . . miles per hour. You have reached the ship's maximum speed.

The altimeter, still winding backward with alarming speed, warns you there is no time to spare. Quickly you adjust the trim tabs and, with a firm grip on the stick, begin the backward pressure—easily, steadily. It requires all your strength, for it is as if a million giant gremlins were pulling against you. First you feel it in your feet, then you know you are rounding out. They weigh tons. (Sometimes your shoe laces are snapped like threads, so much blood is forced to your bottom extremities.)

Next you feel your pants being pressed tightly between you and your seat. Then comes the blackout. A yellowish, murky veil creeps up before you. No use trying to fight it off, once it starts. Just try and keep flying until it passes. The yellowish murk thickens, becomes black; then you are stone blind, behind an ebon black wall.

In those interminable groping moments you yearn fervently for it to pass and for daylight to return. Then two dark discs begin to spin before your eyes, shine, disappear, and light comes once again. Taking stock, you find that you are leveled out and the ship still is in one piece. You knew it would be all the time!

That evening, when you reach for your first refreshment, you notice that your hand trembles. You suddenly realize that you are scared—now that it's all over. The grim and stark possibilities of the death that might have been yours shock you. The spectre of your fellow test pilots who were not so lucky haunts you.

Impatiently you yell for another drink, steal a surreptitious glance at your lovely, gay wife, across the table from you, then curse the waiter for his dawdling.

You've got to steady your nerves before she notices that you've cracked up!

AUF WIEDERSEHEN

NONE OF THE three soldiers looked up. Elbows on the ship's railing, their eyes were fixed on the yellow-green water that sloshed with little sucking sounds between the hull and the wharf. Trailing the threads of their lives in the occupation of Germany behind them, the three soldiers had come together, unknown to each other, here on the military transport, *General Rose,* which a few minutes from now would cast off from the dock and slip down the Weser and into the North Sea and point her bow for Brooklyn—and home. Though their eyes were fastened on the same uninspired scene, their thoughts were as different as three worlds apart.

Peter Dahl, the tallest of the three, a fair, blond boy with an open face and honest blue eyes, was thinking of Gisela. He silently and bitterly cursed the army and its incomprehensible, baffling sea of paper work. But for one single sheet of paper, which had failed to make its devious and leisurely way through bewildering channels, she would be here beside him now, going home to Minnesota as his wife. He was contemplating leaping over the railing to the warf beneath and running to her.

Eddie Weston, the second soldier in line at the railing, was the smallest of the three—in fact, Eddie was usually the smallest individual in any crowd. He had smooth black hair, which he combed frequently with a small comb he carried in his inside jacket pocket, and a thin black mustache which he caressingly stroked with a forefinger. He was from a Missouri farm, and before being drafted had never had a mustache or carried a pocket comb or cared if he was undersized. But

179

since arriving in Germany, and having made the exciting, if slightly belated, discovery of girls, he had become conscious of a lot of heretofore unnoticed things. He was thinking of the many Fräuleins he had had and cursing the army for sending him away from this wonderful land of easy pickings. He thought with avidity of the redhead he had met last night. She was a particularly nice dish. A little more time and he would have added her to his long list of "had" girls. If only he could see her tonight! He, too, was thinking about jumping ship.

Grover Saunders was not thinking about jumping ship. His every thought, every nerve was straining for the ship to get moving; the moments of delay were years of anxiety pulsing through his body. He wanted with all his might to put Germany behind him. Why didn't the ship start moving, get going? He craved to put Bremerhaven—and Frankfurt—behind him. At the thought of Frankfurt his stomach seemed to turn over. He wondered if the body had been discovered yet.

Peter Dahl lifted his eyes from the water, said to the diminutive soldier beside him, "Boy, I sure hate to see this ship pull out!"

"You ain't just a-whoofin'!" said Eddie Weston. "I was thinkin' about jumpin' over this rail and takin' off. I got some *ve*-ry important *un*finished business to take care of—right here in Bremerhaven."

Grover Saunders scowled at the two. "You guys nuts? What's holding up this scow, anyway!"

"What's eatin' him, I wonder?" Eddie said to Peter.

Peter's eyes took on a grave look. "It's sure tough on Gisela. She came up here from Nürnberg, all packed and ready to go to the states with me. They told me back at the base that everything would be cleared by the time I got here. There was just that one last little stinking paper—something between the German officials and the Consulate."

"Yeah, they can sure fug a guy up all right. Tough luck, pal. I ain't about to get married, especially to none of these

Fräuleins. But if I just had one more chance at the redhead I had last night I'd sure feel like I was for a while anyway. Yeah, a guy can sure get fugged up!"

"My folks will be awfully disappointed," Peter said. "My mother is expecting Gisela, got everything all prepared for us when we get home. That damn one little piece of paper!"

"You guys are nuts!" Grover Saunders said. "Why don't this ship shove off!"

The three soldiers fell silent again, and looked down at the water beneath the hull and the wharf. "What I could do with that redhead!" Eddie ruminated reverently.

"NOW HEAR THIS! NOW HEAR THIS!" The three soldiers, and everyone else on the ship, turned their faces toward the horns of the ship's loudspeaker. "Due to mechanical difficulties there will be a twenty-four hour delay in departure. Passengers will be disembarked and military buses will transport them back to the Staging Area."

Peter and Eddie looked at each other joyously, slapped each other on the shoulder. Grover Saunders shook with rage and frustration, gripped the railing, until his knuckles showed white. "Don't take it so hard, pal," Eddie said. "It's only one more day. Tell you what, come along with me, I'll have my girl get you a date."

"Look," Peter cut in. "I've got an idea. You fellows stick with me. Nobody can get out of the compound without a pass. If my marriage paper is in, maybe I can get you two out. They know I've got to have witnesses. I'll tell them you're relatives, or something."

"That'd be better'n the way I got out last night," Eddie grinned. "What you say, fellow? Shall we stick with Romeo boy here?"

"No. Leave me alone. Wait! It's better than being alone. Then we can all come back to the ship together, can't we?"

"Sure, why not!" Eddie gripped him by the arm reassuringly.

In the bus Peter Dahl told them his story. He had met Gisela through her father, who was a German draftsman employed in the engineering office where Peter was assigned. Peter liked the efficient, unassuming and friendly Herr Schmitt. One Saturday afternoon, when they both had worked overtime, Peter offered to drive him home in his jeep. Herr Schmitt insisted that Peter come in for a cup of coffee. Gisela, a student at Heidelberg, was home for vacation. Peter had had two years at the University of Minnesota and so they immediately found many mutual subjects of interest. Thereafter Peter became a regular visitor at the Schmitt home, and soon fell in love with the attractive, brown-eyed, intelligent and unspoiled girl. They talked everything over with Gisela's father (her mother had died in a bombing raid in the very last days of the war), and Peter initiated the papers with the army and Gisela started the required action on the German side. They would complete their education together at Minnesota. Everything went well, if painstakingly slow, except the final paper, on the army side. The officer in charge had assured Peter that it would come through in time and promised to send it forthwith to the Adjutant at the Staging Area in Bremerhaven. Gisela was staying with an aunt in the city these five days.

"Up to the time I had to go aboard the Rose, it hadn't come," Peter said dejectedly. "I sure hope it's there when we get back to the compound. It's my last chance."

"Leave it to the army to foul a guy up," Saunders commented.

"Yeah," Eddie said. "They sure screwed you, Romeo boy."

Eddie and Saunders waited outside the Adjutant's office while Peter went in. Eddie was extremely doubtful that Peter could get passes for them. He spent the next three-quarters of an hour speculating on ways and means to get out of the compound after dark.

Peter finally came out. His face was beaming with joy.

"It came! It came!" He waved a paper covered with official-looking stamps at them. "And look!" He held up three passes. "I don't know what I told them, I was so excited. But it worked!"

Outside the gate Eddie stopped them. "Look, guys. Let's make some plans. Old Worry Boy here—what's your name, pal?"

"Saunders. Grover Saunders."

"Saunders and me, we ain't got no real business with you, Peter, until tomorrow at the chapel. Right? You let us know what time to meet you there and we'll be on the dot. Meantime, *I* got some *un*finished business with a redhead. I'm gonna take Saunders with me. My girl'll fix him up with a cutie. O.K.?" He took out his comb and pulled it through his dark, thick hair.

"O.K., but you fellows be sure and show up at the chapel tomorrow at noon. Don't foul me up."

"I thought we were going to stick together, and go back to the ship together," Saunders said with a tone of disappointment.

"We got no time to watch two love birds on our last night in Germany! Come on, Saunders. We got *un*finished business . . ."

The early fall darkness had descended when Eddie and Saunders turned into the court where Eddie had left the redhead of the night before. He led the way up the stairs and pounded on her door. Upon seeing him she uttered a little sound of surprise. "I thought you were leaving for America today."

"The army gave me a reprieve—just for you, baby. This is Grover Saunders, my pal. Saunders, this is Gerda. Got a friend for my pal? Boy, does he need cheering up!"

Gerda didn't look pleased. "I—I'm afraid I can't. I have to work."

"You didn't tell me you work. Are you a night waitress? Call up and tell 'em you won't be there. Baby, this is our night—compliments of the US Army."

"I'm sorry. I can't. I was just leaving when you came."

Eddie turned to Saunders, spread his hands in a deprecating gesture. "What d'ya know 'bout this dame? The army pulls a miracle. We got time on our hands—and this Fräulein says she got no time for us!"

"Let's go," Saunders said, disinterested and impatient.

Eddie took the girl firmly by the shoulders. "Look, Gerda, baby. We'll go with you wherever you work. If it's a restaurant, we'll eat. If it's a dance hall, we'll dance. If it's a bar, we'll drink. But we'll be there when you get off, and we'll expect you to have a friend for my pal here. O.K.?"

The girl hesitated a moment, then became thoughtful; the ghost of a smile played on her lips. "How you fellows fixed for money? Did you turn in all your marks?"

"I got traveler's checks," Eddie said eagerly, scenting a change in the girl's plans. "I can buy some marks."

"I got marks," Saunders said. "I didn't turn mine in."

The smile came to life on her red lips. "All right. You fellows come with me."

Gerda took the soldiers to a two-storey house at a corner of a street behind a church, not far from the docks on the river. Although it was now completely dark, her finger found the bell with deft familiarity. A tall, stout and affable-looking woman opened the door a crack and peeked out. She had a fringe of dyed auburn hair and wore large horn-rimmed glasses. "*Liebling!* It's you!" she cried, as a bar of light fell on Gerda's face. Then she opened the door wide. "Oh!— you've brought some gentlemen friends. Come on in."

The woman led them to a large living room. There was a yellow, green and blue imitation Oriental rug, a brick-red couch, a huge pink lounge and other odd pieces of furniture.

The shutters were closed and shone as if they had been varnished. Gerda made the introductions. "Frau Zammitt, this is Eddie Weston and Grover Saunders. They're leaving for the States tomorrow, and want a little fun. They've got money."

"*Wunderbar! Das ist schön!*" Frau Zammitt exclaimed. "Will the gentlemen have something to drink first?"

"Bring some cognac, please," Gerda said, without consulting the soldiers, "And coffee for me."

Eddie stood on the balls of his feet, fingering his thin black mustache, surveying the situation with the air of a little Napoleon. "So, baby . . . this is where you 'work'? Sucker me, huh! Why did you let me waste my time last night?"

"Don't be mad, Eddie. You can't blame a girl for putting forth her best foot first. Relax and enjoy yourself."

Frau Zammitt appeared with a tray containing a bottle of cognac, glasses and a pot of coffee. She set it on the coffee table which stood between the brick-red couch and the pink lounge. She asked, "Shall I send in some of the girls now?"

"By all means!" Eddie said, rubbing his hands.

Frau Zammitt disappeared and almost immediately three girls came in. One was a slender blonde with a large mouth and a Roman nose. Her face was made up almost as flamboyantly as a show-girl's, and she wore large gold earrings through pierced slits in her ears. She had on a pink house dress and high-heeled slippers and absolutely nothing else; her bare legs seemed in need of a shave. Her large soft breasts mushed around visibly underneath the flimsy house dress. The second one was a shapely brunette with a square face and a short hair cut. Her skin was coarse and she was hardly made up at all. She wore a short red skirt and a flimsy halter to match; her midriff was bare, and whenever she moved about her pink navel rolled up and down on the little rubber tire of flesh between the halter and the red skirt. She resembled in a grotesque way the motion picture version of a

western saloon girl, which effect she undoubtedly was trying
to achieve. But the sloppy house slippers she wore destroyed
the entire illusion. She gave the impression of having recently
come from the farm. The other one was a smiling, cheerful
girl of about eighteen or nineteen with an oval face, full red
lips and dark wavy hair that fell almost to her shoulders. She
was round and solid through the middle, but had well-formed,
if somewhat stout, legs and thighs. She wore a short, tight-
fitting black velvet dress, which by virtue of its extremely
low-cut neck revealed bulging white breasts. It was obvious
that she, too, had on absolutely nothing underneath the dress.
She was at once charming and exciting.

Eddie said, "Well, Saunders, old boy, take your pick. As
for myself, I'm sticking with Gerda."

"Don't rush me," Saunders said with a little smile, for
the first time showing some interest in what was going on
around him.

Frau Zammitt came in. "Gerda," she said in a quiet voice,
"Anna has been asking for you. Will you go in and see her?"

"My girl friend," Gerda said to Eddie. "She's sick. Excuse
me for a few moments, will you?"

When Gerda returned Saunders was getting into the spirit
of the party. The girl with the black velvet dress was sitting
on his lap, chatting merrily. Occasionally she would throw
back her head and laugh, at the same time clasping her arms
around his neck and drawing his nose and chin into the recess
of her large bosom. He seemed to be enjoying it. Eddie had
turned on the radio and was dancing with the slender blonde.
His head came barely up to her chest. She was holding him
tightly and his head was pressed against her mushy breasts.
The music stopped just as Gerda came into the room. Eddie
playfully slapped the tall blonde on the bottomside. She
giggled. Going over to Gerda, he paused and pinched the girl
in the short red skirt high up on the thigh. She cried, *"Au!*

Hau ab!" He laughed and flung his arms around Gerda and tumbled on the lounge with her.

"Change your mind while I was gone?" she teased.

"Not on your life, baby! After last night's gyp you owe me a lot of lovin'. Come on, baby. What're we wastin' time for. I'm gonna be on that boat for nine long days. I ain't lettin' you out o' here tonight! Come on, baby! Time's a-wastin'!" He pulled her off the lounge. She led him down the hallway.

Eddie awakened to an insistent pounding on the door. His face was embedded in a mass of red hair, and his arm flung over a bare shoulder that shone white in the darkened room. "Eddie! Eddie!" Saunders was calling urgently through the door. "Wake up, Eddie!"

"What's up? What time is it?" Eddie asked, opening the door with one hand, pulling on his trousers with the other.

"The sick girl. I think she's dying. It's three o'clock. We got to get out of here!"

"Anna!" Gerda cried. She jumped out of bed, flung on her wrapper, and ran down the hall to Anna's room.

Then Eddie heard her, a long supplicating moan, followed by a piercing scream. "Hurry, Eddie!" Saunders urged in a nervous voice. "We got to beat it. We can't stand no trouble."

Gerda was back before Eddie could get dressed. Her face was grave, her eyes alarmed. "Eddie, it's her time now. The baby's coming. We've got to do something."

"Saunders and me are gettin' out, baby."

"No, Eddie! You can't! Do something, please!"

"Send for a doc. We gotta get out o' here."

"Christine has gone for the doctor. Please! We've *got* to do something. The baby won't wait."

His army sense told him to go, to get out of there—quickly, but his common country sense told him he couldn't. So he found himself being pulled down the hall and into the girl's room. Her face was livid and her eyes wide with suffering. As the pains mounted she bit her lip and whimpered. She

flayed and tossed from side to side on the narrow bed, kicking
the bed clothing off on the floor. An extraordinary pain rose
within her, she slashed and fought wildly, rolling off the bed.
Eddie picked her up and placed her gently back on the bed.
Then he began to rub her arms and try to quiet her.

"Eddie, we got to go," Saunders said behind him, but there
was doubt in his voice, the urgency had gone out of him.

"We can't leave her," Eddie said calmly. "It's too late."

So he proceeded to do for the girl what he had done for
cows and mares and the other animals back on the farm in
Missouri. When the doctor finally arrived, Eddie was holding
in his wet, sticky hands a wrinkled little monkey of a baby
that was squalling in its desperate, frightened, tiny voice. The
doctor took over, pronouncing what Eddie had done a good
job.

The two soldiers sat on an old stained stone bench in a little
park across from the gate, where Peter would be coming to go
to the chapel with Gisela. The sun was high when they had
left Frau Zammitt's but they still had a little time to kill. They
sat there on the bench in silence, each lost in his own thoughts.
Finally Eddie broke the spell.

"You know, Saunders, seein' that little baby born was something. I've seen pups and calves and ponies—but never before
a human being. Why do people suffer so much more 'n animals do in giving birth? I wonder if they die harder, too."

Saunders shot him a nervous glance. "What's keeping Peter?
We got to get aboard the Rose—remember?"

"Did you see the look in that girl's eyes when I showed her
her baby? I saw that same look once before, in my mom's
eyes, after I fell off the barn. When I came to I was in the
house, in my bed, and the people in the room—the doc, my
mom and some more people—were all quiet and serious. Later
I found out they thought I was goin' to die. The look in my
mom's eyes was wild and terrible. It was a sort of mixture of

grief and hope, like she was seein' both death and life at the same time. That girl Anna last night, she had the same look."

Saunders' eyes were on the toes of his shoes. "Yeah, I know what you mean," he said in a low quiet voice. "I'm glad we didn't run away like I wanted when I heard the screaming. I was scared at first, Eddie. Say, did you notice how the little fellow came all covered with blood. It was all over your hands, too. Then suddenly you were holding a little head, then shoulders, arms, and feet. And when he started to yell I wasn't afraid anymore."

"I been settin' here thinkin' about my mom, Saunders. It would just about kill her if she knew what I been up to since I been in Germany. Just because the girls here seem easier, I thought it my bounden duty to sleep with each and every one of 'em. Back home I never looked at girls like that. If I go on this way it won't be long before I won't be worth the powder it'd take to blow me clean to hell. I'll tell you something, Saunders, I'm through with this stuff. When I get home, I'm gonna be just like I was before I landed here."

"Yeah. He was born in blood," Saunders said, still looking at the toes of his shoes.

Gisela was, as Peter had told them, beautiful, well-bred, intelligent, in a word—charming. The chapel was deserted, save for the three soldiers, Gisela and the chaplain. It was a quiet and beautiful ceremony. A pink blush stole over Gisela's cheek and neck when the chaplain pronounced them husband and wife. Eddie and Saunders kissed the bride, congratulated Peter. "Now we can all go back to the ship—and home," said Peter.

"Yeah!" Eddie said.

"Yes." Saunders said.

When they reached the chapel door, Saunders drew Eddie back inside. "We'll be along in a minute," he said to Peter and Gisela. "I got to talk to Eddie."

They sat down on a bench at the rear of the chapel. "I got to talk to somebody, Eddie," Saunders began earnestly. "I—I killed a guy in Frankfurt night before last. I didn't mean to do it. He kept coming at me and it was him or me. You see, I got a girl, too. A nice one like Peter's."

"Lucky guy," Eddie said. "Well?"

"I took her out to a little place I knew on the outskirts of Frankfurt. It was my last night and we were going to have a quiet good-bye dinner together. Then this big sandy-headed fellow came in. He was with two other guys and they had been drinking quite a bit. He saw me with Hannelore and began making insulting remarks about German girls who go with GI's. I didn't pay any attention to him, and it seemed to bother him that I didn't. Then he began throwing insults in German at Hannelore. I got up and went over to the bar where he was and told him to cut it out. He looked around the room and saw I was the only American in the place, then he really got noisy. He began to say a lot of things to make the other Germans present think he was a big shot. He kept shouting at me to go home. 'Get out of Germany before we run you out, like we intend to run the rest of you foreigners out!' he railed. 'You Amis didn't beat us Germans! We've never been licked! You got no business here, eating and living off us. Get out while the getting's good!' And a lot of stuff like that.

"I didn't want any trouble, so I took Hannelore and we left. There was no taxi outside, so we decided to walk down to the car line. As we were passing a dark lot where some bombed-out buildings were, the three of them jumped me. I don't know how they got there, unless they cut across the back yards and came through the alleys. I loaded into the lot of 'em, caught the first with a good blow in the stomach and he crumpled to the ground moaning and cursing. Then the big, sandy-headed fellow came at me with a knife. I ducked into the wrecked building and tried to hide. I didn't want any trouble.

Hannelore had run away when they first jumped me. The other guy was picking up the one I had knocked out.

"The big guy came into the building looking for me. I grabbed his knife arm and we were going round and round, when I saw the others coming to help him. I knew I had to do something quick. I don't know how it happened, but I got the knife, and stood the three of them off, told 'em to go away and leave me alone. The big one dived at me and the blade of the knife went right between his ribs and into his heart up to the hilt. I never knew a knife could go in a guy's chest so easy. He dropped like a sack of flour. I tried to pick him up but he was stone dead.

"I went back to my base, and didn't tell anybody. I was leaving next morning and figured I'd get away and nobody would ever find out. I didn't even try to see Hannelore anymore. But I know now I got to turn myself in. I guess the MP's are looking for me by this time."

The two soldiers sat in silence for a time. Finally Eddie said, "Yeah, I guess you gotta turn yourself in."

"Yes. But first I've got to see the chaplain."

Eddie Weston and Grover Saunders shook hands. Eddie went out the door into the sunlight. Saunders went down the cool, quiet darkened aisle between the pews, toward the chaplain's office.

Peter and Gisela were waiting in a cab. Eddie climbed in with them. "What's with Saunders?" Peter asked.

"He won't be coming with us."

"But—but what did he tell you?"

Eddie's finger was traveling along the line of his sleek black mustache. "He told me . . . he told me I ought to shave this thing off."

"Didn't he say anything else?"

"Yes. He said 'Auf Wiedersehen.' "

THE END

A NOTE ABOUT THE AUTHOR

James Wakefield Burke has done enough, seen enough, and experienced enough to be able to offer his readers a valid guarantee for the authenticity of the stories contained in this volume. He was born in Tennessee, a descendant of the famed British statesman, Sir Edmund Burke. He started gaining attention as a track athlete, specializing in the 440 and 880 yard runs. He was never beaten in his native South, became a member of the crack team of the University of Southern California, and later competed under the colors of the Illinois Athletic Club and the Newark A. C. A stunt pilot at the outbreak of World War II, he became a Test Pilot for the Army. During the course of the war he tested over 2000 P-47 Thunderbolt fighter planes. Despite the best efforts of the planes, he survived to become a War Correspondent, arriving in Berlin as *Esquire's* War Correspondent in 1945. He has been there ever since. In the meantime he did a stretch as Public Relations officer for Generals McNarney, Clay and Howley. Since 1948 he has been a Staff Correspondent for the Indianapolis *News;* his articles have been syndicated through approximately 100 other leading city newspapers. In between he has managed to appear in many nationally known magazines.

Mr. Burke is married and has a four-year-old son he calls "Dickie."

Since coming to Europe Mr. Burke has gone in for sports cars; his sleek lipstick-red Alfa Romeo and his yellow and blue Ferrari were familiar sights on Germany's Autobahns. He once drove across the Russian Zone, from Helmstedt to Berlin—a distance of 102 miles—in 66 minutes, which is probably a world record for crossing the Russian Zone.

He began his career as a successful best-selling novelist in 1950 with "The Big Rape" which was followed by "Fräulein Lili Marlene," "Three Day Pass—To Kill," "Of a Strange Woman," and "Wrong Side of Paradise." Burke is at present working simultaneously on two other novels.